A Single Mother

Mary Simmons

Contents

Prologue

5 years ago

Jayla - " Look over there, he's hot," Crystal - " where....
yea." Jayla - " Go talk to him." Crystal- " um..... oo kay.

Crystal

I walked in the direction of the blond haired stranger,
I was tipsy but I wasn't drunk atleast that's what I told
myself. I said hi to him, he said hello. I asked him what
was his name and he said Jay, he was around 6 feet tall
and I was 5 feet 4 inches so I had to look up to see his
face, I looked into his eyes and said can we go back to my
apartment. I said sure although something was telling
me no, don't go.

We went to my apartment and he said let's have some
fun he lifted me up like I weighed nothing and brought
me to my bedroom. I only slept with one guy before
and it was my ex he cheated and we broke up. The
next morning I woke up, I had a slight headache, then
I remembered that Jayla and I went to a party yester-

day night. I looked down and I was naked in my bed I looked over beside me and saw nothing, then it hit me, I brought a man home last night.

I got up and looked around for the condom when I didn't see anything I went to the bathroom thinking he might have deposited it in there. I went to check and nothing was there. I started to panic so I called my bestfriend Jayla.

The next day we went to the store and got a pregnancy test I took it and it said that I was pregnant. I told my parents 3 days later they said that they didn't want a grandchild from me at this age and that I brought shame upon the family. I still went to school with my pregnancy whe i was 6 months I did school online until i gave birth.

Chapter 1

Present day

Crystal

I'm on the phone with Jayla, I told Emily. I gotta go Jayla I need to take Emily to school, bye. I hung up the phone and went upstairs, I had already bathed Emily. Let's get you dressed sweetheart, Aunty Jayla will pick you up this afternoon, after school, because I'm working a little later at the hospital today I have a lot of clients today but I promise I will get home before bedtime.

After dropping of Emily at school today I went straight to work. When stepped through the doors of the hospital I went straight up to the receptionist desk sighed myself in and went on my way to see my first patient.

Through out the day I had 27 patients. The 26th one though came into ER with a broken leg. She was a girl though and she was really nice. We're letting her stay for a week. My shift was over 8:15 and I got home 8:30 with a little traffic. When I got home I saw Jayla and Emily on the couch watching TV, she must have showered already because she's wearing pink princess pyjamas. When she saw me she got up and ran towards me screaming mommy. I smiled and picked her up holding her in my arms. Her bed time is 9:15 so that should give me a little time to shower and get ready, so headed to my room to get ready.

I came out wearing my favourite gray night wear. I told Emily it was time to take her daily vitamins and get settled into bed. When she was finished Emily, Jayla and I want to Emily's room. She ran and flopped onto her bed then I turned on the night lamp, because she doesn't like to sleep in the dark, tucked her in and started reading her book for tonight. About 10 minutes later she was fast asleep so me and Jayla step out of the bedroom and went into the living room to talk. I thanked her for taking care of her while I was working later than usual. Something has been on my mind since seeing by 26th patient I told Jayla. She asked," What happened? Do you know her? Is she from college or highschool?" I told her it was none of those. I said she reminds me a bit of Emily. Do you think you know who has a sister?" well I don't know. Have you seen any family for her there?" She said. No, I have seen any family member or anyone that looks like they could be related to her. She has green eyes like his but her hair is a darker blond than his. "What happened to her?" Said Jayla. She has a broken leg, we're keeping her for a week. Maybe a family member or members will come look for her, but I'll keep an eye on her. She's really nice though and me and her get along quite well. I think she has a liking towards me.

Next day

I got up and me and Emily got ready for the day. After school she gets dropped off at a centre. It's a good place. They help the kids with homework, they have fun and they feed them. My work usually ends at 6:20 when I'm not working later. Today just 15 patients are on the schedule. Before my luch break I checked on the girl I found out her name is Cindy Cole. Well it's not like I know his full name anyway, I only the name ' Jay ' which he gave me, he was so drunk I don't think he even remembered his name. I went searching for him a week after I found out I was pregnant, but no one knew who 'Jay' was. I don't regret giving birth to Emily, she's an intelligent, incredible, kind, sweet and funny little girl. My little girl. My little chicken nugget. I love her.

2 Days Later

I went to check on Cindy today and when I entered the room my mouth went dry when I saw who was in the room with her. I haven't seen him since he knocked me up in college. I doubt he recognizes me, he was pretty junk when shit happened. I would never forget his face. Emily has his blond hair but it's curly like mine, she has my olive skin, and she has his green eyes, they pretty much looks the same. I went over to Cindy and we started talking and she introduced me to him, her brother, Jess better yet 'Jay' Cole. I gave him a cold hello and finished my conversation with Cindy. When we were finished I walked out of the room, i had other people to examine.   After I picked up Emily and we went home, I showered Emily made dinner then I called Jayla to tell her what happened. She asked me if I'm gonna tell him. I told her I'm not sure yet and that I don't even know if I even want to acknowledge him.

   2 weeks later   Jayla, Emily and I went to Whole Foods to by groceries. Emily and Jayla went to the ice cream section to to pick out chocolate ice cream and popsicles. I went to the fruit isle to get some strawberries, pineapples and some other fruits. I was walking looking at the fruits when I bumped into him 'Jay'. I went stiff for like a millisecond. I noticed he was wearing black Jean's and a buttoned up shirt. I calmed down and said sorry my tone was cold. He said, " Hi, aren't you the doctor from like 2 weeks ago?" I said yes with a small smile. I couldn't hold it anymore so I asked him if he remembered me from almost 5 years ago. He was quiet then he answered no. Then I said you don't remember the girl you knocked up

at a college party 5 years ago. " Knocked up?" He said. Knocked up I confirmed. Just in that moment Emily came running and saying " mommy we got the ice cream. " He looked as if he just saw a ghost, I'm sure he sees the resemblance. "Okay let's go baby,"I said. He held my wrist stopping me from going but he didn't say a word, so I said here I'll give you my number and name, you can call me I said reaching for a piece of paper in my purse. I wrote my name and number and gave him the paper. I then walked off with Emily and Jayla.

Jess

The beauty handed me the piece of paper then walked away with the little girl and another woman whom I'm assuming is her friend. I'm still stunned, I'm allowing myself to soak in the words she just said. I have a daughter? I have a daughter. The woman has long black curly hair, blue eyes and olive skin. She looks beautiful. The little girl has back length curly blond hair the same shad of mine with green eyes like me and olive skin like her mother. I snapped out of my trance and went to purchase the food I had.

When I got home all I could think about was the girl and the women I had just met. The girl did look like me. I was probably junk when I got her pregnant because I find it hard to believe I forgot such a beautiful woman like her. I have had many flings and one-night stands but

I've only had 2 girlfriends in my 24 almost 25 years of life. The last girlfriend I had cheated on me with one of my cousins, whi envy me. I'm the CEO of Cole industries. I own many business. The woman is a doctor. I looked in my pants pocket and took out the paper. I looked at it it said her name is Crystal Mayers. I then saved the number she gave me in my phone.

I called Jeremy, A guy from my tech-research department. I told him to get me information on Crystal Mayers, he then said he'll send me the info in about 15 - 30 minutes.

Crystal

We went back to my house after we checked out. It was a Friday night so we decided to get some snacks, and basically have a girls night.

Chapter 2

Jess

The next day I woke up early which was strange because I usually am not a morning person. I took my
phone from the nightstand, which was plugged in, and
I looked at my notifications and saw that I had gotten
an email from Jeremy. It was information on Crystal.
After reading the report I got out of bed and headed to
the bathroom to get ready for the day. Since today is
Saturday, I decided to put on some Jean's and a black
and white cotton striped button up shirt. I grabbed my
phone then went into the kitchen. I sat at the white
marbled island in my kitchen and decided to call Crystal.

* this is how I imagined the kitchen*

I went into contacts and typed in her name the clicked
the call button. After 3 rings she answered. "Hello, who
is this?" she answered. "Umm this is Jess," I told her. She
said," Okay, What do you want?" I told her that I wanted

to talk to her and asked her if she was free at 4pm today. She said," I'll ask my friend if she can keep Emily then i will give you an answer." And with that being said she hung up.

Crystal

I called Jayla asking her if she would keep Emily at 4pm today till about 5:30 and she said she ain't got no plans I told her thank you and then she asked why, I told her that Jess ' Jay ' wanted to talk to me. She said he better not want custody or reject her she said coldly. At that moment I froze. I didn't think about the fact that he might want to take her away from me. I haven't told Emily about him yet.. She's a very smart kid and I know she she would be okay knowing that her father doesn't want her. I will fight for her, and we will not get her if he decided he wanted custody.   I took up my computer, went the living room and decided that I am gonna Google him. I typed Jess Cole into the search bar and waited for information to come up on him. I saw a website that said one of the youngest billionaires. So I found out he owns Cole Industries and he's one of the youngest billionaires at the age of 25. His birthday is on October 4th. That means he is about 1 year and a couple months, almost 2 years older than me. I'm 23, I'm turning 24 in April this year, so not too far from now.

Jess

She called me back about 20 minutes after she hung up and said yes, her tone was different from when I called her almost cold with a hint of anger and nervousness. I figured she must hate me but after that party I moved away from New York and went to LA so I could take over the family business. I have a half brother and sister my dad died when I little and my mom had to handle the business about 2 years after my dad died she met my brother and sister's father Charles Marriott. I want to meet Emily, I think that was her name, though. Crystal seems like a good mother. I couldn't get her out of my head last night though. She was really beautiful, her skin looked so soft, her pink plumped lips, full breast and ass. I really don't know how I forgot her. I'm gonna make it up to her and I want to be in their lives. I don't know if Crystal will allow me into her or Emily's life but I hope so, I think she will allow me to bond with Emily.

Chapter 3

Crystal

It's around 3 when I started getting ready, he told me to meet him at cafe Soladochè, which is 20 minutes from where I lived. I decided to where something trendy but classy.

I then fixed my hair and slipped on some white shoes and grabbed a simple black purse . At 3:35 Jayla came through my door, she is my bestie and she has a key for my house, ever since I had Emily she has always been there for me even when my parents turned there back on me. But I finished college and now I'm a great doctor.

I work at hospital that mostly high-end people come to so my I have nice salary and it allows my child and I to live comfortably. I haven't talked to my parents since I told them about me being pregnant, they haven't even seen Emily yet. At 3:40 I got into my car and went to Cafe Soladochè.

I arrived about 2 minutes after 4 and went into the cafe. As I walked in I scanned the cafe to find Jess. I saw him at a table near a bookshelf in a corner. He waved me over and I sat down and said hi. He said hi back, he looked a tad nervous.

I turned to him and said in a cool tone what topics do you want to discuss and you you better not try to take Emily away from me as I relaxed back into the chair and crossed my legs.

Jess

I was shocked that she thinks I would take Emily away from her, guilt washed over me as I thought about it she has been taking care of Emily. I looked into her eyes and she looked back then she said if you want a paternity test I've already set one up for next Tuesday. I said alright and told her I would be paying for it she nodded her head then a waiter came over and asked us what we would like. He was obviously checking her out as if I wasn't here but she didn't seem to notice him and I felt a pang of jealousy I wanted to knock him out cold nut she isn't mine, she's the mother of my daughter.   I honestly knew deep down that Emily was mine, she looked very much like me. She ordered a vanilla lotte with chocolate chip cookie and I ordered an ice cappuccino . He wrote it down then walked away. I asked her when is Emily's birthday and she told me January 18, which means I've already missed it because it march.

I can't help but look at her she's captivating and that outfit makes her curves stand out. From time to time I would see guys staring at her. She told me a few things about Emily. I asked her when I could meet Emily, She said maybe next week Wednesday with an unsure tone. I said look I want to be in you guys lives give, let me prove that I want to, please I asked her. She stayed quit for some time then let out a sigh then said fine.

I was happy she said fine I can't wait to meet her. At 4:50 she told me she has to go so I bid her a goodbye and she said bye. I watched as she walked out the cafe looking stunning and beautiful. I am determined to be apart of their lives.

<h1 style="text-align:center">Chapter 4</h1>

Crystal

Today is the day that we get the DNA results back, deep down I think he knows Emily is his there is no doubt where resemblance is concerned. I've been thinking since he told me he wants to meet her so I'll tell him that he can come with me to pick her up from school her school ends at 3 and that's my luch time, so I'll allow them to meet.

At 2:30 I text Jess the name of the place and told him to get there by 3. It takes 15 minutes to get there so I left 2:40, because I plan to let them spend the rest of the day together I decided to work and 40 minutes extra.

When I got there he was pulling up in his black Mercedes while I was pulling up in my red Audi. I got out and walked towards him at the door then we walked in together i went up to the receptionist desk with him behind me, and asked about the results. She told me that the doctor will come get us in 5 minute and gestured aover to a waiting area telling us to sit.   Five minutes later a female doctor walked out of room and asked for us we got up and went into the room with her. We walked in and she told us to sit we at thenshe pulled out 2 documents handing one to him first and shamelessly flirted with him, I ignored them and waited for her to finish fliting with him and get back to her damn job. He opened it and looked at it. Je was stunned, sat there for like a good minute, I don't think he wanted a kid, so because he just found out he had I decided to give him space.

Once he was done being stunned, I told him that he could come with me to pick up Emily. He looked over at me and gave me a small smile.

Jess

I opened the document and looked at it, it confirmed what I knew, I just wanted assurance. After I was done being in a stunned state she asked me if I wanted to come with her to pick up Emily.

We walk out of the room and through the door leading to the car park. She got into her car and I got into Maine, waiting for her to lead the way. As she pulled out of the car park I remember how she looked. Emily looked like me for the most of it, except for her olive skin which she got from her mother. Just thinking about Emily's olive skin got me thinking about Crystal and how soft her skin looked and I had a flashback of the dream I had over the weekend.

Within about 20 minutes we pulled up to kindergarten, it looked nice, its about 40 to 45 minutes away from my house. We got to the school and Crystal came out of her car and walked towards the school I was walking behind Crystal when Crystal said Hello Miss Gurder. The woman who liked like she was in her early 50s said Hi back and said Emily is in the waiting room. Crystal turned to me and said since she knew she was gonna let me meet Emily, she told her teacher to let her wait in the kids area with the other kids until she came.

Walking into a room, I spot Emily, she was playing with 2 other girls. She looked so happy and sweet. Crystal walked up to her and said hi baby, I miss you so much. Then she gestured for me to come over. I walked toward her and Emily then I said hi Emily. She said hello in a cute and shy voice while hiding behind her mother.

Crystal said this is Jess pointing towards me, and he is um... my friend. She came from behind Crysat and waved at me. I asked her if she was hungry, she nodded and I said what would you like to eat. A smile came across her face as she said pizza. I looked at Crystal and she nodded. Crystal said why don't we go to Papa John's then. Emily had a huge smile on her face, she looked very beautiful. I said let's go then and Crystal and Emily got into Crystal's car and drove away with me behind following them.

Chapter 5

♥

When we arrived we walked in together, scanning the room I found a booth, with Emily in my arms I pointed over to the booth and we walked over. Emily looked over at Jess and game him a smile, he looked at her at gave her back a smile. Then he started asking her how was school, what was her favourite colour, food and movie. She told him that her favourite movie was Cinderella and that she liked to dress up and have tea parties with her dollies.

I told them that Emily could spend the rest of the with Jess, and they both smiled at me I was glad that they were getting along and Emily seemed to like him. I told him that I was gonna pick her up at 8:20 and that he should text me his address. I stood up, hugged Emily and kissed her on the cheek, then I told her I loved her then looked to Jess and said to him that he better take care of my baby else I'm gonna kick his ass and walked out.

Jess

I watched as Crystal walked out the door, she had on black jeans that fitted her like a glove and a flowy green shirt with black boots. She must have left her doctor coat in her car, she looked beautiful and I could feel some eyes staring at her.

5 minutes later me and Emily walked to my car and I buckled her in the backseat then went to the driver's seat and got in. I told her that we were going to the store and the the mall cause we need to do some shopping so she could have stuff at my house. Today is gonna be an eventful day.

First stop, the grocery store. We got there I unbuckled Emily, the we walked in the store with her holding my hand. I asked her what kind of food she wants. She said we should buy strawberries, chocolate vanilla ice cream, gummy bears, lemonade and some snacks. First we went to the snacks aisle and she picked up a bunch of snacks she said those were her favourite and then we went off to buy other stuff.

After we were finished with groceries, we went back to the car, I placed the stuff in the truck then buckled Emily in the seat. We got to the mall and bought all different kinds of stuff, we bought some toys and clothes. I asked her if she had an iPad. She said yes but her mom was gonna buy her a new one since hers is old so I took her to the Apple store and I bought her the newest iPad and a pink unicorn case that she has chosen.

Twenty minutes later we have arrived at my house which is pretty large. Tomorrow I'm gonna call the interior designer to come and decorate a room for Emily. I clicked the remote control for the gates that are attached to my keys to open the gate then I drove up into the drive way.

I climed out of the car, then took Emily out and we walked to my door and then I opened it. When Emily walked in she said wow in a cute voice. I think she likes my house, she turned towards be and said yowr howse is beawtiful. I looked over at her and smiled then I picked her up and brought her to the living room. I turned on the tv and clicked on Disney channel. I told her not leave the living room and that I'm gonna take out the bags out of the car. She smiled at me then turned back to the tv.

Five minutes all the bags were in the living room. I took up the bag with the ipad then unboxed and helped her set it up. I then looked for the bag with the food and went to the kitchen to unpack the bag.

I went back in the living room and asked her if she was hungry, so I took her up and carried her to the kitchen. I packed her in a chair then opened the fridge and took out the strawberries. I asked her if she likes peanut butter. She said it's not her favourite nut she'd eat it. So

I made her a peanut butter sandwich with strawberries and orange juice.

After she finished eating I asked her if she knew how to swim she said no. I opened the bags until I found the swimsuit I bought and 2 arm floaters. I changed into swim trunks and we headed to the back yard. I has 2 towels with me and I rested them on the lounge chairs. I had a projector so we could watch movies in the pool and I played a princess move while we sat it floaties.

About an hour later I bathed her and changed her into some PJ's and then i ordered some Chinese food for dinner. After i fed her we went and the sofa and i turned on the tv while we waited for Crystal to come pick her up in about 20 minutes. I enjoyed today. It was nice to hangout with my daughter. I'm so happy Crystal allowed us to spend time together.

Chapter 6

Crystal

When work was finish I took out my phone and looked at the text with his address then I typed it in my GPS. I arrived at his house 25 minutes later and called him to let him know I was here, his house is huge. I'm a doctor with a well paying job, I don't really see the use of living in a mansion, there's too much space but I won't judge you if you have one.

The gates opened and I drove in. I parked then got out of my car and went up to his house. I waited for a few seconds before the door opened and I saw Jess. I said hi and he gestured for me to come in, he then walked me into the living room where I see Emily. I walked up to her and said hi baby and sat down beside me, she said hi mommy and jumped up to hug me j hugged her back and smiled at her before she crawled in my lap. I asked her how was her day.

She said it was fun and that he took her shopping and they went to the pool and watched Cinderella. I said that's lovely baby, you ready to go. She said yes and Jess walked off, a few minutes later he came back with her stuff I took them from him and said thank you.

He told me that he bought her a new Ipad, I told him he didn't have to because I'm planning on getting her a new one soon but thanked him anyway. He said that he knows. I told him goodbye and went to but Emily's bags in the car, then I went back to the house and picked up Emily, I then brought her out to the car and buckled her in her car seat then went to the driver's seat the drove away.

Jess

I watched as she walked with Emily down to her car and buckled Emily in. I wondered what it would be like if we were a family. shit. I've never even thought about a family before I met them. I don't even know if she likes me much more want a family with me. We do make beautiful children and I'm definitely attracted to her.

That night I lay in my bed thinking about my daughter's mother and if we would ever get together. I do like her and I'm gonna get her.

Crystal

We got home about twenty-five minutes later. I gave Emily a bath and made spaghetti and meatballs after we were finished eating Emily went to bed then I hopped into the shower, a few minutes later I got out of the shower and got dressed then went to bed. I thought about how good Jess was with Emily, he's hot yes but I don't think if we got together it would work and I don't want to give Emily false hope that she would have her family living together and happy.

Chapter 7

Jess   Today I'm hanging out with my friends there are 8 of us in total;me, Tylor, kyle, Kira, Nate, Mace, Scarlet and Ray. We all own our our companies, Scarlet and Mace are my cousins and Scarlet and Ray are a thing, Kira and mace are married and have 2 kids and Kira is pregnant with their 3rd child and Taylor and Nate are engaged while me and Kyle are single.

I'm not denying that I am attracted to Crystal but I don't think she likes me. I wonder if she has a boyfriend and with that thought my hands turn into fists and a rage passes over me and I don't know why, I'm not jealous, I have no right to be, she's not mine.

Ugh, I need a distraction. Maybe it cause I haven't got laid in a while at this point its bin 2 and half weeks since I've been with someone and since I've met Crystal and Emily.

It's now 6 and I'm going to the club with my friends at 8 so I headed upstairs to my room to get dressed. I picked out a black shirt and pants with a brown jacket and black leather shoes.

It was now 8:05 and my friends and I are in the bar section of the club. This club is owned by Ray, we go hangout there sometimes, it's our hangout spot.
Kira is sitting and bitching about how she can't drink and it's not fair yada yada yada. That's when I saw her Walked in.
Crystal   Jayla convinced me to come to this new bar she found with some of our friends. I really didn't want to come, she called a babysitter to stay with Emily. She said I'm going even if she has to drag me there because I need a break. I gave in and then we went tk my closet where she started rummaging through my clothes.
She suddenly stopped then squealed, I knew she found something and I probably wasn't going to like it. That's when she pulled out a black silk dress that had a low cut and a slit running up the side.

The dress is beautiful I just think it's a bit too much for me. She came running towards me with the dress and said "oh my gosh, you have to where this. You have the body for it and you would look totally sexy." I looked

over at the dress and signed in defeat because I knew j
wouldn't win.

I went to the bathroom, took a shower, washed my
hair and shaved. After I was finished with the bathroom
I went over to my bed took up the dress slipped it on
and then placed some blak shoes on my feet.

Jess had already had a shower and she brought her
dress, she was in my closet looking for some shoes to
borrow. After j was finished she came out wearing a red
dress that was thigh length and she was wearing my red
bottoms.

When we got to the club, we showed our ID's to
the bouncer and he let us in. I could fell the gazes of
men watching as we walked towards the table with our
friends. They all looked great. There were Gio, Luke,
Charlotte, Melissa, Hayley and Hayden. I sat in the end
with Hayley and Jayla sat beside Luke

Luke and Jayla like each other but they're oblivious to
mother's feelings. I keep pushing her to confess to him
but she's too nervous and chickens out.

Charlotte, Gio and Melissa went to the bar to collect
our drinks.

Jess

I don't think she sees me. When she walked in she was with the girl I saw her with when we met in the supermarket. She was in a silk black dress with a slit that went to her thigh.

I could just sense all the men looking at her, and that had me livid she has a beautiful body so why would this bastards stare, but she's mine. Hold on did I just called her mine, well she is the mother of my daughter, in some way she's mine. They sat at a table with a couple of people, which I'm guessing are her friends.

There were six of them. Three men and three women. I saw a man with dirty blind hair and hazel eyes look at her. He was there ogling her and that put a mad expression on my face.

I turned around to see Mace waving his hand infront of my face, I turned towards him hs said " bro I've been calling you for like the last two minutes what the hell is wrong with you." I shook my head before mumbling out nothing. They al looked over at me like I had three heads. I growled a what and they Scarlet said ooooo someone's mad. I turned to her and rolled my eyes and they all started laughing.

I decided I might as well tell them about Emily and Crystal. Guys I have something to tell you. They all sobered up from laughing and turned to me. I said I have a daughter and they all gasped and looked at me as if they just saw a unicorn popped out ice cream on my head. I told them the story of what happened.

Kira was the first to recover from her shocked state and asked when are they gonna meet her. I told them soon and that I was having her on Saturday.

I pointed over to Crystal and said you say that woman, she's Emily mother. Everyone looked towards her, kyle said damn she's hot. I glared at him and he started to laugh. Mace turned to me and said you like her don't you. I looke at him for a bit then shrugging my shoulders. The ladies squealed and said ooooo. Will ray looked at me with a smirk on his face and kyle said well you're not saying no.

I said and I'm not saying yes. The next time I looked over at her I saw that they were gone, I let my eyes searched through the club and saw them on the dance floor.

Crystal was dancing when a man came behind her and started dancing with her. Jealousy and rage flowed through my veins. He then started grinding on her, she looked uncomfortable and tried to push him back but then he only came closer to her and held on to her hips forcing himself on her. Before I knew it I was walking towards them.

Crystal

I was dancing when a man came behind me soon he was grinding kn me. I was uncomfortable table sk I tried to push him away but he came closer towards me and forcefully grabbed my hips and forced himself on me. Then out of no where I fet his weight come off me and I sighed in relief then I turned around to se Jess. The man was on the floor with blood coming out of his nose.

Jess had dislocated his nose. I looked up at him in shock, His features were parched with anger. Before I even registered it his hands were holding mine and he dragged me out of the club.

Chapter 8

Crystal

When we were in the car it was dead silent. I was angry at him, he had no right to do that although I'm glad he helped but I'm fully capable of kicking his ass. I spent three years up until junior year in highschool learning karate.

A few minutes when we were on the road he asked me for directions to my house breaking the thick tension in the air. I don't know what his problem is, he and I aren't even a thing. Sure he's the father of my daughter, but he isn't much more.

Emily doesn't even know that he's her dad. I'm thinking of telling her soon, once I know more about Jess and he and Emily gets closer. I think we'll bring her somewhere nice and tell her there.

When we got to my house he parked the car and sighed, his anger is now gone. I opened the door and came out then closed it and walked up to my door but before I could reach my door I felt him grab me by the arm and spun me around ti face him.

I - he started but I cut him off. I told him that it was okay and not to di it again then sighed, opened my door, walked inside and close it in his face. I stood by the door long enough to hear him curse under his breath but I herd it.

Jess

When she closed the door in my face I knew she was still upset. I just couldn't stand there and touch what is mine. Hold up, did I just call her mine.

I walked back to my car and sat in the seat. I just sat there for a while, pictures of Crystal flowing through my mind.

My mind wondered to my friends. I knew I wouldn't hear the end of it.

~2 weeks later ~

Jess   It's been two weeks since me and Crystal have had a whole conversation. When I look for Emily, she just says no more that three sentences. I think she's distancing herself from me. Today Emily is going to meet my friends. I think they'll love her.

After I picked Emily up from Crystal's house we went to my house, all my friends are there waiting to see her. It's the weekend so Emily is staying with me. I took her out of the car seat and grabbed her bag then we went inside.

Everyone was sitting on my couch in the living room even the other kids were their, I'm taking her to see my mim tomorrow though. I walked over to the couch with Emily still in my arms and her bag. They smiled at her and introduced themselves one by one.

Once everyone introduced themselves she said hi shyly, I placed her on a spot on the couch beside kira and Taylor. She looked up at Kira and smiled then said she liked her eyes and hair, with that I leave her with them and went to her bedroom to put away her bag.

After putting away her bag I went back to the living room. When I entering the room I herd Emily laugh she was playing with the adults and kids. I smiled seeing that she was getting along with them.

She completely forgot about me at this point and was talking to Kira I think she had taking a liking to Kira, maybe it was because she had kids so she knew how to handle them.

After a few hours we said our goodbyes then it was time for me to make Emily dinner then get her ready for bed.

After she was finished eating I gave her a bath and know I was tucking her into bed. She asked I'd she could face time her mother and I said yes. I then went for my phone. I got back into the room and looked for her mum in contacts then I click face time. She answered on the third ring, when she came into view she looked a bit dazed but I didn't pay much attention.

I passed the phone to Emily and she smiled as she said Mommy. As Crystal was talking to Emily I herd a few noises in the background, so I hopped in bed with Emily and watched as she talked to Crystal.

A few seconds later I saw something move in the background as she was going to end the call. I looked at her suspiciously before I realised a muscular hand touch her but before I could say anything she had ended the call.

I was beyond livid. I don't want another man to touch her. She's mine and only mine.

Crystal

For the past week and a half I've been seeing this man called Brent. I haven't got together or even kissed anyone since I found out I was pregnant. I wasn't going to have sex with brent I haven't known him long enough to do that.

I don't let male figures could romantically be involved with because I don't want Emily to get attached.

When Jess called we started kissing a few seconds pryer. I didn't know he was going to calm, before he did Brent was going to leave and he kissed me, I was still in shock.

Chapter 9

Crystal   Today I'm picking up Emily from Jess, I know it's gonna be awkward because of the accident that happened on the phone. I'm pretty sure he saw Brent. I haven't really been getting any type of feelings for him maybe we need some more time to get to know each other. I don't wanna do it with him yet because I don't feel a thing. Yes, he's attractive and nice but we don't got a connection. So im7thinking of breaking it off.

****

I parked my car in his drive way then hopped out, I walked up to his front door and pressed the door bell, I waited a few seconds before the door opened and there stands Jess and Emily. This weekend I'm planning on tell Emily that Jess is her father. I smiled at Emily and took her in my arms. Jess told me to come inside and sit while he go and gets Emily's things. He came back about two minutes later with her stuff in his hands. I asked him if he could help me bring them to my car.

He walked behind with Emily's stuff in hand and Emily in my arms. I placed Emily in her car seat while Jess placed her stuff beside her then I closed the door. I then turned to him and said that I was gonna tell Emily this weekend about him being her father, I also told him that we were going the tell her at Chuck E Cheese and to meet us around 1:30 there. I then told him bye and got in my car before he had a chance to say anything else incase he was going tk ask me about Brent.

Jess

She got in her car and left before I had a chance to ask her about the man I saw in her house when Emily face timed her the other night. I was happy that we were finally going to tell Emily about her being my daughter and me being her father. I was not happy about Crystal talking to other men I wanted to be the only man she talks to I don't want another man to touch what is mine.

For the next two days I would be away in Italy on a business trip. Franko Romero wanted to do a deal and was going to tell me about what he had in mind. People always wanted tk make deals with me because I have one of the most successful businesses in the world.

****

Crystal

Today is the day were telling Emily, at the current moment we are getting ready to head out the door. Emily's wearing black pants, shirt and a leather jacket with pink Adidas shoes and her hair is braided in two while I'm wearing a white leather skirt with a silver ring as a zipper and a black graphic t that is tied in a knot at the front and black leather boots.

We arrived there a few minutes later at exactly 1:32 PM. I grabbed my purse and went to the back seat to get Emily out of her car seat. As I was walking towards the front of the building I saw Jess standing there wearing a whit button down shirt brown khaki like pants that are rolled up with white shoes and shades. He was looking delicious damn it Crystal stop thinking of him like that you are still not cool with him remember.

I walked up towards him and he asked me if I'm done checking him out with a smirk on his face. A grown made it's way on my face and I ignored him and said let's go inside. I walked up to the counter with Jess in tow. There was guy at the counter and he was shamelessly checking me out I internally rolled my eyes and said Hi, I made reservations under Mayers. He checked the computer then walked us to the table he said he will come back with a waiter.

I looked over at Jess to flashes of anger in his eyes I ignored him then asked Emily what she wanted, she said she wanted. She smiled at me and said pizza I then turned to Jess and asked if he want pizza too. I asked if we should get cheese and Emily said yes while Jess nodded.

Two minutes after that the man from the counter came back with a waiter and then left us with a waiter. I smiled at him and said hi, mag we have a large cheese pizza please. He nodded his head while scribbling on his notepad then excused himself .

After he left and turned to Emily, I asked her If she wanted to play the games when she was finished and she grinned up at me then turned to Jess and asked if he will play with us. Jess smiled and said yes princess.

I then turned tk Emily and asked her if she remembered when she asked me about her father she said yes them I pointed to Jess and said he is your father we , met again at the grocery store and asked her I'd she remembered. She smiled and then said yes then she turned to Jess gave him a huge smile while saying dada. I smiled at them both and Jess lifted her up and placed her in his lap and then he play with her and was talking to her.

Five minutes later the waiter then came back and placed the pizza along with a couple of plates on the table then asked what we wanted to drink. I ordered apple juice for Emily and ordered a strawberry smoothie for me and Jess just said water, I said thank you to the waiter with a smile and he blushed and smile back at me. He looked a little younger than I maybe he was in college.

The rest of out time here went nice and then it was time for us to return home so we said bye to Jess, then grabbed my purse and with a sleeping Emily walked to my car. I placed her in the car seat, hopped in my own and with that I drove home.

Chapter 10

Jess

It's been about 3 days since I last saw them. Today I'm going to text Crystal and ask her if we can meet up. I'm going to try and have a conversation with Crystal and tell her it's because we need try to be civil for Emily, that will give me a reason to get to know her.

I texted Crystal and she said we can meet up tomorrow because she had a day off I'm taking the day off tomorrow as well I can do that anytime I want because I'm the boss.

I noticed Emily likes painting and drawing, art in general so I went to the mall and picked out an art set as a gift, hopefully she likes it, I miss her little smile.

I have never thought I would have a child but I love her, we do talk a lot and we have gotten closer, I wanna be an amazing father to her. _______________________________

It's the next day and I've already gotten ready for the day, we agreed on meeting at 10:30 am at the mall.

Women usually throw themselves at me I've gotten use to it but I realized that I haven't even looked at them the only woman that's on my mind is Crystal.

We are now at the mall and crystal looks nice in her jersey shirt and shorts and my baby looks so cute in her yellow Micky mouse shirt and shorts.

^ CRYSTAL'S CLOTHES

^   '

Emily said that she wanted to got to Build a bear so we went with her and she made a brown bear with a blue dress with bees on it and matching head band she was so fascinated with the process of making it it was nice to watch her. Although we haven't known each other too long I'm super attached to her and I love her so much.

After walking around and shopping we decided to go to a family like setting food dinner and ordered milk-shakes and burgers. While in we we're talking I realized we look so much like a family and I smiled to myself at that fact. A few minutes later one of my old flings saw me and came over she was flirting with me and asked me if I wanted to meet up tonight or some other time. Before I answered I glanced over at Crystal and saw her features changed she was clearly annoyed, she was trying to hide it too but I guess she's not good at hiding it.

I turned back to the girl, Channel I think her name was she's a model, she has blue eyes blond medium length hair and a tall lean slender body of course she was beautiful but she didn't compare to crystal, I looked at Channel and told her I'm not interested in anyone right now her face changed, she was mad, she walked off and didn't said a word.

After she left Crystal was back to normal she was playing with Emily I looked at them and smiled i wonder what it would be like if we had another child. Where the hell did that come from, I brushed it off and we engaged in more conversations until we were done eating.

We went wondering around the mall until we saw a trampoline place, Crystal suggested that we go, Emily was jumping up and down she seems excited so we went. As we got inside Emily ran away and crystal and I hurried after her. Crystal took of hers and Emily's shoes and I did the same and put them in the shelves near where we are. Emily was jumping up and down with me but crystal didn't go, I went to her and told her that she should come in with us as she was watching Emily she nodded her head then went beside Emily.

Emily asked Crystal if she could do some tricks crystal paused a little thinking then she said sure baby, Crystal then stretched a bit then she started doing some crazy flips, I was astonished, I didn't know she could do those things and I kind of turned me on June wondered what else she could do I shook my head as she finished and heard clapping there was a crowd watching her she smiled and went to talk with Emily while asked her if she could show here, I looked around and saw some men staring at her I mean she's beautiful, smart, I now guess flexible and I don't know what else she can do but I plan to get to know her.

Chapter 11

Jess

I slowly opened my eyes as the the sun is shining in through my windows, I then turned over to my bedside table to look at the time on my phone, today is Friday ant it's currently 9 AM. I'm going to see my mom today and bring Emily with me I left my employees to do their work as I will come in later to see how everything is.

I checked if I had any messages or calls then I got off my bed and went to the bathroom. I brushed my teeth washed my face and took a shower, after I was finished I went into my closet to pick out something casual but formal.

I went down the stairs to the kitchen to make me some coffee after I was finished with my coffee I grabbed my keys and went to the garage, I decided to drive my black sleek Bugatti.

I knocked on Crystal's door to see an amazing sight, her in some sheer black pajamas, I took in the sight before as my eyes wandered down her body, under my intense gaze she shivered but quickly recovered and moved aside so I could enter. She excused herself to put on a robe although I don't mind her in what she was currently wearing.

This is my first time in her house so I looked around a bit, it was very fitting for a child to be in but I had to say she had great decor taste. She came back wearing a black robe and she had Emily's hand in her along with a backpack for Emily.

I watched as she kissed Emily good bye, my mind started thinking about how her lips would feel on mine they're plump, soft and pink, so kissable.   I shook my head to get those thoughts out of my mind, I waved crystal good bye and Emily went on our way.

We were meeting my mom at Sun and Moon cafe we are getting breakfast and Emily would get to interact with her grandma.

We got there sometime latter and I unstrapped Emily and put on her bag for her. We then began walking towards the cafe. I spotted my mom and walked over to her she immediately took Emily up and said " Look how adorable you are my grandbaby. " She the kissed her know the forehead.

Soon we all began talking and Emily shocked my mother with how intelligent she is. They seem to get along together. An hour and 35 minutes later we said our goodbyes and I brought Emily back to her mother.

I got to Crystal's house knocked again and she came out in this beautiful blue mid thigh dress it hugged her curves and this time I couldn't control the desire and lust I felt for her so I waited until Emily went to change and put away her things.

I wrapped my arm around her small waist bringing her closer to me as her eyes widened in shock. I said "Do you know how sexy you look in this dress, you're making it hard for me to control my self, darling. " Her breathing quickened as I pressed my lips against hers passionately with a hint of Possessiveness.

Her lips tasted so sweet it was addicting, possibly the best kiss I ever had. I pulled back just in time when Emily came running into the living room looking away from Crystal's shocked state I kissed Emily on the forehead and bid them goodbye before cloning the door and getting into my car to drive to my company still thinking about the kiss.

Chapter 12

Crystal

Since we had the kiss I could not stop thinking about him. Why did he do it? I keep asking myself. As well as does he like me? I carried on with the rest of my week before it was time for him to see Emily.

It was now Friday and he's picking up Emily, I've been nervous all week. I don't like him so I don't know why I'm nervous. I got Emily ready and packed her bag while She was watching TV. Right as I was finished putting every thing in her Cinderella bag I heard a knock on the door so I went towards the door and look through the peep hole. I do this as a safety precaution, I wouldn't be able to forgive myself if anything happened to Emily.

I saw Jess so I opened the door. When I did he looked straight into my eyes not looking away a flash from what happened last time went through my head and I was in a daze for a bit. I shakes my head stood back and allowed him to enter. I walked way from the door leaving him and went over to Emily. I told her it was time to go and told her to ho put on her shows and socks while I went and got her bag.

As I bent over to get the bag I felt a presence behind me, I turned around quickly looking up into Jess's eyes. It was like I couldn't move. He had put his arms around my waist and pulled my closer. I heard Emily's footsteps and quickly pulled away and pushed him back.

I gave Emily her bag and got away from Jess, he was looking at me with a weird look in his eyes. I turned away from him and kissed Emily and carried her out to his car while he followed closely behind.

Jess

I really couldn't stop thinking about her, I was happy to see my daughter but I wanted to see her mother as well. I'm going to tell her my plans to court her but I'm gonna need Emily's help.

When we got home I opened the door for her and helped her out while I grabbed her bags. I opened the door for her and we went inside. She took her bags and ran up to her room. I thought she must be hungry so I went to the kitchen I made her some peanut butter and bread with strawberries and bananas until she came down stairs. A little while after I placed the food around the table she came downstairs with her Cinderella plush doll.

As she ate I went to change in sweatpants and a hoodie and I also grabbed blankets, I bought a huge Cinderella blanket for her and I wanted to surprise her with it because she loves Cinderella. I hid it behind me and went up to her she was almost finished with her food at this point. I called her name then pulled the blanket from behind.

She got off the chair and ran towards me, she was smiling, I loved seeing her happy. I wish I was there for her earlier days, to see her first steps, hear her first words, all of the struggles and happy moments. I'll make it up to her.

We went to the theater with the blankets and the pop-corn. The movie we chose was her favorite"Cinderella". As I sat there is saw how happy she was and for a second thought of how happy I make her life ;my phone rang, I picked it up and was surprised to see it was Crystal. I answered;"Hey is everything ok" she asked in a worried tone,I assured her everything was fine and we talked for five minutes about Emily and then I decided let Emily have a nap,I did the same. I heard my door open so I went to check expecting Crystal,it was her

Said he came in and sat down looking exhausted,I gave her a glass of water and we talked. I tried to confront her about the kiss we had but she quickly changed the topic to Emily;she asked me "Where is she?" I told her she's sleeping and she went to her room to check on her As I stayed in the living room thinking. She came back to the room and sat next to me, alot was going through my mind at this point ;"I couldn't stop thinking of you after that kiss" we both said nervously.

We looked at each other with wide eyes. After a few seconds I asked her if she was willing to give me a chance, a chance for us to be a family. She looked at me then looked down as she thought about what I had asked her.

After about a minute she said sure why not. I was so happy, I had a huge smile on my face. After about fifteen minutes she was getting up to leave;just before she went out the door I grabbed her hand,turned her around leaned in and.... "Daddy?"are you awake?.I woke up to Emily tugging on my shirt,turns out it was a dream.

Chapter 13

♥

Crystal

Lately I've been thinking alot about these feeling I think I might possibly have for Jess. I don't want us together and we might break up and be parents that are nasty exes. That will just brink too much drama into Emily's life. I don't want her to have parents that can't get along with each other and have a bad or toxic relationship. I don't want to fall for him cause I'm scared if things go bad I'll end up hurt and we'll probably have a bad friendship if we were to be friends after.

I picked up the phone and decided to call Jayla and asked her for us to have a girls' day with Emily and go shopping, get our nails done, get some food and go swimming. She said yes and now I'm going to get us ready.

I went to Emily's room to see her on her bed with her iPad playing a puzzle game, I told her we we're going to have a girl's Day with aunty Jayla she said yay and went to her closet while I stood and watched what she picked out. She took out a black and white striped shirt with gray, black and white plaid skirt with white and black fur slippers. It looked nice so I let her ware it because it was a good outfit choice.

I helped her put it on then went to my room and picked out a blue and white checked coat with a whit T-shirt dress underneath with a white Michael Kors never full hand bag and white boots.

I then packed a big with snacks, water, slippers for me, scocks for My baby, and other things. I then went to the closet in the living room hallway near the door to get her stroller. I put everything by the door then went to check in Emily. I found her still in her room so I told her to bring her iPad and I grabbed my phone. We went to the door and I opened it then placed the stroller in the trunk of my car.

Once I was done getting everything in the car and strapped in Emily, I got into the driver's seat and told Jayla that I'll meet her at Mark Lonning Mall. We got there 37 minutes later. A little after I parked I saw Jayla's silver Audi park next to me. I got out and we greeted each other with hugs. I then opened the door and got out Emily and gave her to Jayla. I went to the trunk and got out the stroller. While Jayla strapped in Emily I went over to seat beside my driver's seat and got out my bag.

About a minute later we walked into the mall with me pushing the stroller and Jayla holding both of our purses. We decided to first go to a shop called Kate Jane. It is one of my favourite stores. As we walked in I was a white beautiful dress. It caught my eye so I decided to try it on and it was the perfect fit. Jayla also found a pant suit she liked and I got Emily a little sweater dress that was so cute and this beautiful star necklace, I also got a moon and star one so we would be matching .

After a few more stores we went to Chipotle to get some food then we went to the salon to get our nails done. Jayla and I got similar designs while Emily say between us with her ipad. I don't think a four year old need to get her nails done so I didn't let her. I think it would be more appropriate when she's 10. While we were doing that we discussed a few things to do with Emily's party that's like in 3 weeks.

Jess

For the past few days I've been thinking about how to ask Crystal out. I'm sure of my feelings towards her and I want to make the 3 of us a family and extended it eventually. I can't wait to do so.

I think I should buy her some blue, red and white rose like 12 dozen of those, show up in a nice outfit, probly get a plane to come write it in the air and have some candles on a path way and ask her. I think my plan is solid. I hope she feels the same or is willing to try this out, atleast for Emily's sake.

For the whole day I've been planning out what I will do it's about 7:38 now and I am going to text her and aske her if they're at home. I'll use the excuse to see Emily although even if she says no. I will be visiting Emily.

I texted her and she said they're home. So I got dressed into a whit button up shirt and gray and white plaid pants with black shoes.

I called the pilot to make show he was ready as I headed out. In about 45 minutes I was there and the pilot was about 10 mind away. I got the people to set up the flowers and candles while I waited for the pilot.

~Imagine it being so etching like this but at night ~

The pilot would be in arriving in 2 minutes, so I hurried out of the car and went to knock on the door. Crystal answered, she was in sweat pants on a red crop top. She looked cute with her hair in a messy bun. I heard the plane so I smiled said hi and pulled her into the drive way. Her face looked surprised and shock. Then right when she was about to say something the plane came writing will you go out with me, I pulled her into me and turned her towards the plane.

After the plane went she was quiet for a while, thinking of what to say. I was there a little nervous waiting patiently for her response. After like 2 minutes she smiled and said sure. Then she frowned and said but we have a few things to talk about first. I was confused but followed her into the house.

I told her my true feelings towards her, she said she likes me too but she says she's worried about the outcome if something goes wrong. I didn't think about that. I didn't want us to have a bad relationship if this doesn't work out.

I was still positive that it won't and convinced her. I then told her when to get ready and an outline of what she should wear, because the date would be a surprise.

After talking, we watched TV together in the couch coddled up in blankets. It was a warm sight, I wanted it to be just like now.

Chapter 14

Jess

It has been 2 days since I asked her out. I decided not to do a basic boring date I want it to be special so I came up with setting up a cliff movie picnic kind of set up. So I found a secluded cliff Forrest area with a little water fall river part and I bought a projector for the movie part so I could do the movie and I asked her best friend Jayla to pick out a swim suit for her and I made the food myself which is spaghetti and meatballs and I also made burritos and I bought her favourite kind of cake which is chocolate mousse cake.

I hope the date goes well I packed everything into my car then I got dressed into a green dress shirt with black pants and I texted crystal that I'm going to leave the house.

~ Jess's outfit ~

I locked up my house then went to my red Audi rs7. When I pulled into her drive way I texted her that I was here and then walked up to her door an rang the door bell. Emily opened the door and I picked her up and hugged her. I carried her to the couch and asked where was mommy, as she pointed to the direction of the stairs I saw Crystal coming down it. She looked breath taking and we held eye contact until she made it over to us.

~ crystal's outfit ~

I then placed Emily in the couch and stud up I then hugged her and told her that she looked really beautiful while I gave her a once over and smiled her, she smiled back showing her beautiful smile. Just then Jayla came down the stairs and pushed us towards the door, before she closed it I kissed Emily on her forehead and told her bye and her mom also kissed her told her to be good and told her that she loved her and said bye.

We then walked over to my car and I opened the door open and then went over to my side. I turned on the radio and while I drove to our destination Crystal tried to get me to tell her where we were going and once she realized I wasn't going to budge, we talked about Emily, work and our lives.

When we got there I got out and went to open the door for her. I watched as she looked around then I blind folded her she joked that I was gonna kill her and I laughed. Once I got there I took it of and she let out a small wow as her eyes widened I smiled at her cute reaction while leading her over to the picnic blanket then I but the basket beside us and my bag on the other side of me.

I asked her to pick from numbers 1,2 or 3. She picked 1 which means we are swimming first. Without saying anything I reached into the bag and pulled out or swim-suits. She looked at me and asked how I know her side and j told her a little birdy helped me. She took the swim suit and examined it then a smile curled up her lips and a knowing look spread across her face then she shook her head. I began to remove my clothes and put on my swimming trunks. She looked at me and I looked her confused and asked her what and she said well I can't change in front of you turn around. I sighed then did just as she asked then waited for her to tell me that I can turn around again.

When I did my eyes widened and I checked her out she was absolutely and undeniably beautiful. I whispered mine under my breath. I then grabbed her hand and run towards the edge and we jumped off.

We resurfaced and I wrapped my hands around her waist and pulled her closer and u looked into her beau-tiful eyes. I asked can I and she nodded her head and in one swift motion our lips were touching. It was bliss absolute bliss. I leaned more into the kiss the tapped the back of her thighs indicating that she should wrap her legs around my waist and I kissed her more passionate-ly.

We came apart eventually to breath both of our hearts were beating fast and breathing hard. She then help my face and pulled me in for another kiss which surprised me.

After the kissing we swam around little bit but we got hungry and went up for food. We then eat the spaghetti and meatballs. She moaned saying it was delicious and I started at her intently, he little moan made my little Jess jerked. She looked at me innocently and I shared my head and smiled at her while we were eating we made conversation about basic things about ourselves.

Once we finished I put away our dishes in the basket and I took out the cake she looked at it like it was her last meal and I chuckled silently to myself. I then went to set up the projector. We watched a few movies while we cuddled under the blanket and eat the cake.

She fell asleep before the last 1 could finish and I kissed her on the head and went to pack up the stuff then I carried her into the car on the back seat so she could sleep comfortably then I went and got the things. I then drove her home and she was still asleep so I went to rang te door bell I told Jayla to keep it open while I went to get her. I then opened the car and took her up and then carried her to her bed room I kissed her again on the forehead after tucking her in and went to Emily's room.

I kissed Emily on the forehead and went down stairs I told Jayla bye then left. That night I sat in bed with a full blown grin on my face and I fell asleep with the thought of my 2 girls. Today was amazing.

Chapter 15

Crystal

Today I had work and I was dropping Emily off at Jess's. The date was nice, no one has ever really done something like that for me. Jess has really been sweet over the past few days he texted me all the time, to like how my day was and, how was Emily. When he video called Emi (Emily) I would drop in to say hi. Since he was keeping Emily today and tomorrow, after my shift at the hospital finished later on, me and Jayla are having a girls night.

That means tons of snacks, movies and some self care like painting our nails and face masks. So here I am at the store with Emily to grab somethings for me and Jay's (Jayla) movie night like skittles, popcorn, snickers, hummy bears, gummy worms, a 1 litre bottle of Sprite and snacks. I'm also picking up some wipes, snacks and a bottle of organe juice and apple juice for Emi, I let her pick out some gummy worms as well, i don't like to give her too much candy she hadn't ate some in a while so I let her.

After I got everything I needed I went to the cashier station to purchase everything. After the lady at the check out area was finished I took the trolley with the bags and Emi back to my car. First I put in Emi in the car, then the bags, then I put back the trolley and we were ready to go over to Jess's.

After a few mins I pulled up in his drive was and before I even rung the bell the door opened revealing a woman, if she wanted she could be a model, slim, tall and had a pretty face. Then I see jess behind her and she kissed his cheek. What I was wondering is if she was one of his flings or something, if so why did he take me out that day, you know what, I don't think he wants a relation-ship. Maybe he was just testing the waters.

Anyways I brushed away my thoughts. When the woman walked away, I gave Emily to him and went back to the car to get her bags and then handed them to him. I told Emily that I loved her and kissed her forehead, then went back to my car and drove away. I could see the confusion on his face on why I didn't even tell him bye, then it turned to realization but I had already drove out of the drive way.

Jess

She just drove off after kissing Emily and telling her bye. She didn't tell me bye. I'm confused as to why. Then realization hit me. She probably thought that Maria Cole was one of my flings or something. If so then this might ruin the progress we have going on and I'm worried. I shouldn't have let her kiss me oh my gosh. I closed the door and Emi and I went to the kitchen. I take out strawberries, bananas, pineapples and tangerines, her favourite fruits and out them on the island. While I'm washing the strawberries, Emi takes out her iPad and watch Barbie on Netflix.

Finally after peeling the tangerine, I'm finished with her fruit dish i then put it in front of her and pour her some apple juice. I then bring her bags to her room and tidy up a bit from the last time she was here. My mother wants to spend some time with her so she will be coming over shortly, hopefully everything goes smoothly.

Crystal

After leaving Jess's house I go pick up Jay. I'm a bit hurt over the whole Jess and the mystery lady delema. If he didn't want an EXCLUSIVE relationship why come to me. I need to stop thinking about him. As I got to Jay's house she walks out and she had a whole flipping suitcase behind her. I roll my eyes at her, she's so damn extra. She has a wide grin on her face as she opens door, then she leans over and hugs me and I hug her back.

As we were driving back to my house I told her about the while situation and she was fuming. She was cussing him out she even said he looked like a rat on steroids. I was laughing my ass off. She always makes me laugh even when I'm not in the mood and that is why SHE MY MOTHER F - ING BEST FRIEND.

I was excited about us spendin time together alone and not worrying about stuff so I told her we shouldn't talk about him anymore. We went to my room and out on comfortable clothes.

~My outfit ~

~ Jayla's outfit ~

Honestly we look bomb as fuuuuuuckkkk. We then went to the kitchen to prepare all the delicious snacks and drinks we will use for the night. Last minute we decided to go to Target and dollar store and get a bunch if nail supplies.

We headed to my closet and got Coats and then went to my car and to the store we go. We went crazy going through the isles and picking out stuff. We got packs of nail polish, 2 foot bath things, a foot , the foot file thing, the foot soap and nail oil. We then got some small towels and press on nails

After we got everything we needed we went home. We entered the house with 2 big bags packed to the mass.

We decided we were gonna sleep in the living room with make shift beds. We dumped out everything on the ground. Jayla wanted Chinese so we ordered Chicken Chop Suey with noodles and fry rice for Jayla and sweet and sour chicken with fry rice for me.

As we waited I went to get the water for the foot baths, then we placed our feet in them. After a while we took out our feet and put them on the foot rest platform in the foot bath thing. Then cleaned off the polish, after getting it off when put our feet back. Then we cleaned the white crust off. After doing that we decided that it was now time to paint our nails.

I decided on a coral peach colour and Jayla wanted baby pink. After that we washed our hands and put the press on nails. We used the nail oil an we were finish. When we thought our nails were snatched enough we went to relax on the couch and put Netflix on the TV.

Like 15 mins later the Chinese food finallyyyy cmae. And I was h u n g r y so we dug in. Yayayay the empty void in my life was finally filled lollll.

We watched so crime shows cause why the cheese burger heavens not.

It was like 2 In the morning when we finally finished watching TV and I was tireddd. So we went to bed.

Chapter 16

3 months later

Crystal

Over the past 3 months have been amazing. Jess and I have gotten pretty close and I'm falling, fast and hard. The thought that something might happen that will ruin us has been nagging me at the back of my head. I take a deep breath and shake my head clearing my thoughts.

My Emily has been so happy. Not that she wasn't when it was just us and Jayla but having her dad here she seems more carefree and happier.

I'm just sit ting here in the bean bag chair across from them just watching the beautiful view in front of me. They're sat on the floor and he's playing dolls with her. Bright smiles on their faces and laughter can be heard a few times. I smile at them feeling content I just hope this lasts.

Jess

I can see her watching us. She has a beautiful smile that I just love so much on her pretty face. A few months ago if you told me that I would be here with the woman of my dreams and a wonderful daughter, I would have laughed in your face and told you to check yourself into a mental hospital. That sounds absolutely ludacris.

I continued to play dolls with Em (Emily) then when she wasn't looking at me I started to tickle her. She began to giggle uncontrollable and hearing her joyous sound I chuckled. I could also hear Crystal low laughing while she watches us. I'm not sure what she finds so amusing but I guess I couldn't say anything, I would be a hypocrite, since I often watch her, I watch how much of a good mother she is, and how I can see the love she has for Emily displayed heavily on her face and her eyes gleam with adoration when she looks at her. It's a sight to see.

"Shall we go get ice cream?" I asked them already knowing Emily would agree. She looks at Em before she speaks," Hmmm, sure," She says smiling at Emily. " Not too much toppings though," She says directed at Emily. " I don't want my baby to get a bad tooth or a bellyache," She continues, trying to give Emily a stern-ish look but fails.

"What would you like baby girl?" I ask Em as we stand at the counter in front of the seemingly teenage girl that works at the store. " Strawberry," she answers in her cute little soft voice. " What would you like babe?" I ask turning my head to Crystal. " ummmm... I would like a chocolate pistachio please," she tells the young girl. And the girl nods. " I would like a Vanilla, thanks," I tell the girl at the counter. She nods as she scopes our ice cream. She starts with Emily's then she does Crystal's own and then finally mine. " Thank you," All three of us collectively tells the girl.

After we ate our ice cream we went on a short walk then headed straight home. Emily was tired and as a result I carried her. After a while she eventfully fell asleep in my arms.

Once we got home, well crystal's house, I've been staying over often, I put Emily to lay in her bed then I went to Crystal's room. I opened the door and saw her laying on the bed. I then went over to my side and got in and immediately cuddled her. She smells nice, of Vanilla and citrus. I then pecked her on the lips but as I was pulling away she deepened it and bit my lip.

I groaned in response to the lip biting. She then flipped us over and she was un top of me straddling my lap. She pulled away giving us time to catch our breath.

Chapter 17

Jess

Today I'm asking Crystal on a date night. I already put in place baby sitting for Em (Emily), my mom will be doing that thankfully. I plan on either getting her Lilies and then asking her or just simply asking her. I think I'm a go with the flowers because she deserves them and it's a nice thing to do for her, plus lilies are her favorite.

I grabbed my wallet and the spare keys she had giving me, then went to my car to go to the nearest flower shop that I just Googled.

....

I walked through the aisles looking at the different options and my eyes caught on the pretty pink lilies that were screaming my name. So guess what I did. I picked them up and walked to the florist at the counter and paid for it. I also saw some roses and grabbed a single one, I'll give this to Em.

I'm back at her house now and she has just gotten off of her shift at the hospital, she looks tired but she's cuddling a sleeping Emily. I put the lilies behind my back and hid them in a cabinet while she wasn't looking.

After hiding them I walk over to them and pick up Em then proceeded to carry her to her bedroom. After kissing her head I went back to the living room to tackle mama bear.

I picked her up bridal style then placed a chaste kiss on her forehead then also brought her to her room.

I then sat at the edge of her bed watching her, I know that may come off a little creepy but it wasn't so. I pondered changing her out of her scrubs or just living it on, but I then decided that she wouldn't want to sleep in it, so I changed her.

I got an idea so I went to grab a piece of paper and a pen. I'm going to ask her out using that and then put the lilies un top of it beside her on the bed so when she wakes up she'll see it.

I then went to the dining table with my laptop to get some work done while i wake for my babies to wake up.

~ 3 hours later ~

Crystal

I opened my eyes slowly then sat up in my bed and stretched, trying to shake of the sleep from my awesome nap. As I twisted my body to the other side of my bed I noticed some beautiful pink lilies beside me. A lazy smile seeped onto my face.

He must have been getting them while he was gone, I wondered where he was but not giving it too much thought, then fell asleep with my baby girl. I was incredibly tired from my 12 hour shift.

I then noticed a note under the lilies and I took it up. " Will you go on a date with me my love," It said. I then jumped off the bed and I was on a conquest to find Jess.

It didn't take too long to find him. I found him sitting at the table doing whatever he is on his laptop, I assume he's working. " Of course I will," I say standing behind him. He then turned around with a huge grin on his face and I smiled at him.

" How do you like the lilies, darling?" He asks me. " They're beautiful thank you," I tell him.

" I got a rose for Emily," He says. Hearing this, a warm feeling spreads in strong waves covering my body and I give him a bright smile. " That's really sweet, babe" I tell him as I lean in for a hug.

He wraps his hands around my waist pulling my closer to him. I lean in for a kiss and his lips meet mine. Our tongues danced with each other in a happy manner. His hands go lower gently resting on my bum and I smile into the kiss the same time he does.

It was a blissful moment but we were interrupted by our little Emily. "Mommy, Daddy, What are you doing?" She asks smugly already knowing the answer, That little vixen. Jess and I pulled apart hearing her. " We're showing our liking for each other by kissing," Jess tells her. She nodded her head and smiled with a small smirk resting on her little face.

" Come here baby, Daddy has something he wants to give you," I tell her. She walks over to me while Jess goes to get the rose. Soon he returns, "Here baby, a rose just for you," he says handing it her while he bends down.

" Thank you daddy," she says with a smile on her face. " And this is how a man should treat you when you're older my sweet little girl, not that you will be having a boyfriend until you're 40," He says a stern but playful look.

" If you say so daddy," She rolls her eyes. " Who are you rolling your eyes at young lady?" He asks in mock surprise. " Uhhh... You daddy," she says but it's more of a question.

"I'm gonna tickle you so you better run," he tells her. " Mommy save me," she says running towards me while laughing.

Jess

For our date, I planned a simple picnic garden style. I own a piece of property that has fields of trees and flowers and I had a little lake on it. It was quite a sight for sore eyes. I got my friends to help me decorate it, while me and my mother made the food.

We made Caprese sandwiches, egg salads, and burritos as well as we packed chocolate, strawberries, and cherries. For beverages, we went with smoothies, water and Pepsi.

My mom will be babysitting Emily and they're hanging out with some of my friends and their kids. I bet she'll have a great time with them. She's a friendly little girl and easy to get along with so I don't doubt she will make friends with the other kids.

I'm definitely looking forward to this date. Just some alone time with my beautiful lady. It's 1:30 and she's probably getting ready as we speak. I told her I would pick her up around 2: 20 so we could get there before sundown.

It'll take around 2 hours to get there and as much as it's beautiful at night, especially with the lights I installed, I want her to see it during the day.

I got her friend Jayla to pack a swimsuit just in case we decide to go for a swim in the lake and I had blankets for when she gets cold as well as towels. I think I have everything put together perfectly, so there's no need to worry.

I took a quick shower, then went to my closet to pick out the best clothes for this occasion.

Crystal

Ahhhhh I'm so excited to see what he has planned. He always seems to woo me somehow. I just finished having a nice soothing shower now here I am standing in front of my closet looking at the clothes I have.

I decided to make this process go by faster, I would pick out 5 outfits I like, that will go well for a picnic. He told me that we'll be having a picnic but gave no other information, so I'm relying on Google to tell me what to wear for a picnic.

I got my 5 outfits picked out so now I'm currently analysing which one is the best to choose.

5 minutes later I finally chose. I went with a blue and purple romper and then I paired it with white strap up sandals.

I look at myself in my 6ft tall body mirror. I hum in approval of how I look before going over to my dresser to add some more jewellery.

Jess told me Em (Emily) will be staying with his mom and friends. I haven't met his friends officially as yet but If he thinks they'll take care of our baby then ok. He also told me some of his friends have children of their own so Em won't be lonely in that sense.

I went to her room to see what she chose to wear. She picked out a red frilly shirt and some grey sweatpants with white lines on the side. And for her shoes, she picked out her red and black Vans. It was a cute and comfy outfit so I helped her get dressed.

When I was finished with everything else that I had to do, which entails packing Emily's bag and getting my stuff together, it was 2:15. So I had 5 minutes before Jess said he was coming to pick us up.

We sat on the couch and Emily started playing a game on her Ipad and I scrolled through Twitter, catching up on the latest news or drama Twitter is filled with that.

Jess

I arrived at her house at exactly 2:20. I went up to her door and opened it since I have a key. My ladies were on the couch waiting and I smiled as I approached them.

I bent down and kissed Emily on her forehead then pressed a chaste kiss on the corner of Crysie's (Crystal) lips, Not wanting to give our daughter a show.

"Are you guys ready?" I asked them, even though it was obvious that they were. "Yes daddy," Emily answered while Crysie nodded. I picked up Emily in my arms and Crystal grabbed her purse and Emily's bag.

I opened the back door and buckled Em in her car seat while Crystal placed her backpack on the seat beside her. I then Went to open Crysie's door then went to get in my side.

" Shall we put on some music?" Crystal asked in an awful British accent. Emily laughed at her while aI let out a chuckle. "Yes we shall," I answered in an equally terrible British accent.

For the rest of the ride to my mom's house, we sang along to the songs and laughed at each other. I was enjoying my time with my family. It felt good to say that, and I've been feeling less lonely since they're in my life.

We kissed Emily before leaving and Crystal made my mom porpoise to call if anything happened even if it mos a minor issue.

After getting back in the car, I swiftly captured her lips in a kiss. " I've been wanting to do that the whole day," I say after we pulled away. She smiled at me and then held my hand.

~ 2 hours later ~
Crystal

I gasped as I saw the view in front of me. It was absolutely breathtaking. There were a bunch of trees, beautiful flowers and plants. "It's gorgeous," I said still staring at the view in awe.

" Not as beautiful as you, my love," He says. And that's when I finally turn to look at him, a sincere smile gracing his oh so kissable lips. I give him a full-on grin. " Thank you, baby," I tell him.

"Shall we get our date started, my beautiful lady?" He asks. "Yes we shall, my handsome prince," I say matching his goofy energy.

He got out of the car and then came to my side to open the door for me. He held out his hand for mine and I slipped mine in his. They fit just right. I love how much of a gentleman he is, although he wasn't so when he got me pregnant.

We walked towards a seemingly big blanket that was spread out on the ground. " Wait here, I'll go get the basket from the car," He says. I told him okay, then he went to go get it.

Jess

I came back to see her laying on her back gazing at the sky. She looks absolutely beautiful. I went to the other side then placed the basket in front of us.

Noticing that I was back she sat up. I leaned closer to her and then wrapped my arms around her hugging her. She placed her arms around my neck. I let out a sigh of contentment. We just sat there for a while enjoying the presence of each other.

"Alright, I'm hungry," she says pulling away from me. I let out a small laugh. " Sure let's eat," I say while opening the basket.

"My queen, I come to you with a fuck ton of sandwich-es, as well as strawberries, smoothie, water and Pepsi," I tell her in a funny voice. She giggles at my antics and I laugh along with her.

After we finished eating we talked for a while and cracked some jokes. " Come let me show you the little lake I have," I tell her standing up and then stretching out my hand to her.

   She takes my hand and I pull her up. " wait, did you say your lake?" she asks looking at me confused. " Yup I own the property," I tell her. " oooooohhhhh," she mumbles. " Okay let's go," She says.

Chapter 19

C   r   y   s   -
tal

It's time to make my move. I'm ready to have sex again. I know he's waiting on me and that's why he hasn't made a move on me. The only things we do are kiss, cuddle and hug and It's time to change that.

He's not here right now as well as Emily. He took her to go to a sleepover at her best friend Reign's house. So I decided what perfect time than now.

My plan is to get into some type of lingerie and then wait for him to get back. Even though I haven't done it in years I still have lingerie, I think they're cute and I don't need to have a man to wear such pieces.

3rd POV

Jess opens the door and then begins walking to Crystal's room excited to see her. He opens the door, " Hey ba-," he pauses mid-sentence seeing the scene in front of him.

His eyes widened seeing his girlfriend in sexy, red garments sitting in the middle of the bed looking beautiful as ever. He then slowly walks over to his side of the bed and gets in.

" I - What - uhhhh," he says, unable to speak. " I decided to make the move, and you're clearly in shock," Crystal says, letting out a small laugh at the end. " Do you like it?" she asks. " You look gorgeous, my love," Jess says, his voice dropping a few octaves.

Suddenly the room feels hotter, Jess thought.

Crystal climbs over to him and then sits in his lap, she's feeling bold and is loving his reactions. "Babe, are you sure you're ready?" He asks, " There's really no rush," He adds. " I'm sure," she says looking into his green eyes. Their eyes seem to be having their own conversation.

Crystal leans down and captures his lips in a sensual, passionate kiss. Their tongues fight and their lips smack together. They then pull apart and she tugs at his shirt wanting it off. He gets the hint and lifts up his arms to make it easier for her.

Soon enough she gets his shirt off and then she tosses it to the side. Jess's hands grip her hips and she starts to slowly grind on him. His jeans, that he still had on created blissful friction.

He flips her onto her back switching their position. He then starts kissing her neck, then down to the valley of her breasts. His kisses left tingles in their wake.

Crystal covers her mouth trying to stifle her moans. "Baby, let's your moans out, I want to hear you," Jess tells her.

Jess continued to kiss down her body reaching her pussy.

He then shifted the material that covered her already wet pussy, and slid one of his fingers into her wet, slick heat.

She let out a whimper at the feeling of his fingers inside of her. She arched her back in pleasure wanting more. He then added another finger, making it two.

Soon enough, he began sliding his fingers in a slow paste wanting her pussy to stretch out as it was quite tight. The only thing that could now only leave her mouth are the moans signifying her pleasure.

While his right hand is busy taunting her sweet pussy his left hand went to her breast and began massaging them. Her hard nipples could be seen poking through the material that covered them.

He then stopped his sweet torture to her pussy. " Take it off," He says, the desire clear in his voice.

Crystal then gets off the bed and began to take off the red lace that adorned her body perfectly. She slowly pulled the fabric off her teasing him as he watched her.

His green eyes, now darker than their normal colour glided over every inch of her body that was visible. "Stunning," He said.

He then made a hand gesture telling her to come closer and she obeyed. She was now standing between his legs and his hands on her waist. They just looked into each other's eyes, absorbing their very much so intimate moment.

"I want your dick inside me now," she says in a horse but sexy voice, her want and need for him is obvious. "Baby, there is no need to rush, let me worship your body," He tells her.

He gently pushes her onto the bed, "open your legs for me, love," he tells her and she does just that.

Jess's fingers instantly go to her clit, he rubs his fingers in a circular motion, he presses hard but not too hard and he gradually gets faster.

Screams are on the edge of Crystal's tongue, and it won't be too long before she falls off the edge.

Jess's other hand latches onto her left nipple. He pitches it, but it's not to hurt her only enough to give her immense pleasure.

His hand slid into her wet hole, her juices getting all over his hand. His tongue then goes to her other nipple teasing the pretty pink bud.

Her screams fill the room and Jess smiles, enjoying how good he's able to make her feel.

He can feel she's close to an orgasm and he fingers her faster and harder. Her pussy clenches around his fingers, and he lets out a low groan.

His dick is painfully hard at this point, and it's just begging to enter her beautiful pussy.

Suddenly her moans stop and her cum seeps out of her, his fingers are still in her pussy and they are covered in her cum. She sighs in contentment after she has her release.

He unbuckles his pants and slides his boxers down his long legs.

Crystal's eyes widen at his length, even though it's been in her before when she was 19, it has been years.

"Are you ready, darling?" he asks. "Yes, baby, now don't keep me waiting," she says with a slight smirk on her face.

He slides his length into her easily and that is because she's so wet. She feels so good, he thought to himself. He then began sliding in and out of her and he goes faster as time goes on.

Her breasts are bouncing up and down giving him a lovely view.

They're both moaning at how good it feels for them to be joined. His thrusts get faster and harder and she moves her hips so that they can move in sync perfectly.

All that you can hear is the sound of their bodies against each other and their moans.

Chapter 20

3rd pov

After their wonderful night, the couple woke up cuddled in each other arms. Jess's hands were wrapped around crystal's waist, and their naked bodies were as close as possible as they could to each other.

After talking and doing cute couple stuff, off to the bathroom they went to get their day started.

"Would you like to have a bath with me?" Crystal asked. " Sure love, let me get the water running, would you be so kind to get us some towels?" he asked. " yes I will, kind sir," She responds before running off to fetch some towels.

"Mmmmm," crystal moans as her muscles relax under the warm water. Jess begins to rub her back softly. "

Would you like a massage, Luv?" he asks her. "Yes babe, thank you," she says smiling softly at him.

" What do you think about a family day?" Crystal asks. "Uhh... well... for today?" he asks. " Yup, sure," she responds. " Like going to the park, arcade, zoo, carnival, water park," she continues. "How about the water park," he suggests. " Yeah, oh and the park too," she agrees.

" And we could go for dinner after," he says. " Sounds like a plan," she smiles at him. "When shall we go collect our baby?" he asks. " After breakfast, assuming she's eaten at Reign's," she tells him. "Okay good, I miss my baby girl, not that I haven't had a wonderful time with her beautiful mama," he says with a small laugh.

After picking up Emily, the family retreated to their home, to get ready for the day. On the ride back home Jess and Crystal explained the basis of the day to Emily and she was very excited.

" Let's spend the night at my house," Jess suggested. "Sure baby," Crystal responded.

Jess doesn't like them hopping back and forth between each other's houses. And he plans to get that sorted out real soon.

"Is everyone ready and has everything," Crystal asks. The bags with some added necessities as Crystal and Emily has some stuff already at Jess's place.

"So Waterpark, Dinner then park?" Jess asks. " Yup that sounds about right, what do you think honey?" She asks Emily.

"I think it's fine mommy," She says in her little cute voice.

"Okay then, let's get on the road, it's quite far away, maybe about 3 hours," Jess says.

"The water park is huge," Emily said, her eyes were wide as she looked at it in awe. Crystal chuckled at her excitement. "Alright let's get our stuff and go have some fun," I said.

Crystal

"I'll go to the bathroom with Em (Emily) while you go and change," I say taking our stuff from him. "Okay, love, see you in a few minutes, be safe," he says then kisses our foreheads. He walked towards the men's and I did the women's.

I got Emily changed first, She's wearing a one-piece with cute little strawberries all over it and she looks so adorable. I then got myself dressed, I put on a black and blue 2 piece. We then changed into rubber flip flops. I would always use rubber because you don't slip as much, since the rubber kind of absorbs the water.

When we got out of the bathroom Jess was by the door waiting for us, he looked very much handsome. "You look so cute Em," he says as he picks her up. " You look, beautiful baby," he says looking at me. "Thank you," I say smiling at him. "Now I have to fight off both little boys and men," he says. Both I and Em laugh at him.

"Why are you guys laughing at my pain," Jess groans and we laugh harder. " You're silly daddy," Emily says still laughing at him. "No I'm not baby, daddy's very smart," he says and I roll my eyes at him.

"Do you wanna go down the water slide, baby?" I ask Emily. "Yes mommy, the blue one please," she says pointing at it. "Let's go then," Jess says. "Mommy it's too big, I'm scared," Em says. "Don't be scared baby, mommy and daddy are going on it with you," I tell her.

We wait in line, luckily there wasn't a very long one and there were like 10 people in front of us.

Finally, it was our tourn, I sat down with Em in my lap then jess sat behind me then we went down the slide. Emily let out a little wooo as our bodies hit the water.

"That was soo much fun," Emily says. "Yes baby, it was, should we go swim now?" Jess asks. "Yes we shall," I say.

I get Em's floaty and arm floats out of the bag. Yes, she can swim, but it's better to be safe than sorry, there's no way I'm losing my baby girl.

"Come Em, let's put on the floaties," I say.

After putting them on we went into the pool, it's 5 feet deep but it has shallow parts which is where we stayed because of Em. I don't think she could manage the deeper part.

Suddenly jess splashes me and my hair is wet, my mouth drops while water is dripping down my face. "

No, you didn't," I say glaring at him. "Oh yes I did," he mocks me. Then he splashes me again.

Emily starts laughing at me and Jess is too. "Mommy is gonna kill you," she says. " Oh yes, I am," I say from behind him. Then I hug onto his buck and dunk him into the water.

Chapter 21

Jess

The rest of the day went awesome. After the waterpark we went home got changed then went to the restaurant I booked. We bonded and I'm just really happy that I was able to bond with my girls. God, I love them.

After the restaurant, it was around 7 when we got back and we took a stroll in the park as well as got ice cream. Then after playing with Emily on the playground, we went back to my house to finally settle in for the night. Not long after that Em (Emily) fell asleep, we had a pretty packed day, I'm actually surprised she didn't fall asleep sooner.

Crystal and I tucked her in bed and kissed her good-night and now we're sitting in bed under the comfortable sheets watching Criminal Minds. Over the past few months, I've spent With Crystal I learned that she ab-solutely loves crome dramas.

She laid beside me, snuggled up in my arms. I then leaned down to peck her soft, inviting, pink lips. I sighed in contentment, savouring our little kiss. I haven't been able to taste those lips of hers today as we were out and we don't want to smother Em too much with our PDA.

What was supposed to be a short sweet kiss turned into a long passionate one. I was a starved man and it looks like she missed this as much as I did.

To get into a better position she pushed me down so I was lying flat on the bed, then got on top of me, and she did this without us breaking apart.

I moan into the kiss and she deepens it more, I was not even sure that was possible. She smiled against my lips and then pulled apart. I was in a little daze, after that.

I woke up to Crystal kissing my neck. And boy was I a happy man right now. I would love to wake up like this every day but unfortunately, she's not ready to move in yet.

She then leaves my neck and continues kissing further down my body. I gasped in surprise when she bit my nipple, she starts laughing at me and I took the moment to flip the situation. I flipped her on her back so she was laying on the bed and I hovered over her.

I capture her lips without warning now getting a gasp from her and I smirk. She wraps her arms around my neck and her legs curl around my waist.

"Mommy, daddy," Emily says as she begins to open the door. Crystal and I stopped our intimate moment and fived ourselves under the sheets. "Hey, mama's baby," Crystal says to her. It's a good thing we were clothed and our little moment hadn't gone far.

My little girl is a cock blocker though. Why is she up anyways?

"Why are you up Em?" Crystal asked softly, voicing my exact thoughts. I made a hand gesture for her to come in bed with us.

She climbed up on the bed the snuggled in the gap between me and her mom.

"Uh, I fewt like it" she says as she plays with her little hands. Crystal put her arms around Em bringing them closer and I did the same so now we are snuggling.

"Let's go get breakfast," Crystal says. "Okay mommy," Emily says in her little cute voice. I smile in compliance. I got out of bed and help my hands out for Em to Jump so I could carry her to the kitchen and she complies.

"How about chocolate waffles with fruit?" I suggest. Crystal bites her lip, nodding as she thinks about it. "What do you think baby?"She asks Emily. "Mhmm," Em hums. "Waffles it is," Crystal announces.

"Emily you can go watch tv, Jess, can you cut the fruits up while I do the waffles?" she asks. "Sure baby," I say giving her a toothy grin.

"And done," Crystal says putting the waffles on a plate. "I'll go get the syrup," I say getting up.

"Thank you, " Crystal says as I put syrup on her waffles. "You're welcome, love," I responded smiling at her and she smile back. I then put syrup on Em's waffles and she thanked me.

"Mommy, daddy, can i go to Tilly's house today?" Emily asks giving us the puppy eyes. "I'll say yes, ask your dad," Crystal says. "Sure, baby girl," I say smiling at my little princess.

"Yay, thanks mommy and daddy," she says. "I'm going to go pack my bag," she adds. "Okay baby, let me go call Tilly's mom," crystal says and Em runs off to her room.

"Now that our little princess is gone, let's finish what we started this morning," I say as I pin her to the wall.

"Nope," she says popping the p. She stares into my eyes as she grinds her front against mine. Oh, I see what game she's playing. I pick her up bridal style and put her on the bed.

She sits up a little, leaning back, with her arms holding her up. "Oh really now," I say, my voice low. "Mhmm," she hums still looking in my eyes. Then she flips us so she's now straddling my lap.

"Thought you didn't want to continue what we started this morning," I say smirking at her. She rolls her eyes at me. I grip her ass and she gasps at the sudden contact.

She bites her pink luscious lips and that's all it takes for mine to come crashing on hers.

Chapter 22

Crystal

"I'll move in with you," I tell Jess. He's been asking me to for a while now and I finally agreed. I won't be selling my house though, I'm going to rent it out.

"Ahhh, great," he says grinning at me. He then pulled me into him by wrapping his strong arms around my waist. I smile into to hug. "Are you gonna sell the house or?" he asks. "I'm renting it out, which makes it easier for us as we don't have to move the furniture only clothes and other personal items," I say.

He nods his head at my statement. "How quickly do you think we can get everything in our house?" he asks. I internally smile at the fact he said our house than his. "Hmmm, maybe before the end of the week," I say.

He hums before pulling me onto his lap. "You know-" I began to say but he kissed me. He fixed me better on his lap before deepening the kiss. My eyes fluttered close at the delicate, amazing sensation of the kiss.

I pull away from the kiss and stood up getting up from his lap. "You know the faster we pack, the sooner Em (Emily) and I can move in with you," I say a mischievous smile dancing on my lip.

I didn't wait for his reply but scurried off to my room to get to packing.

I opened the door of Jess's car and got out. Jess and I are currently picking up Emily from her school. We go through the gates and walked into the building the headed straight for Emily's classroom.

"Hello my baby," I say walking over to Emily. "Mommy," she says as I lifted her in my arms. "Hi daddy," she says looking over at Jess. She opens her arms at Jess signalling him to take her. And he complies. "Hey baby girl," Jess says hugging her.

A minute later, Em's teacher walks over to us. She smiles at Jess and gives me a small forced smile. "Is everything okay with Emily?" I asked her as I saw no point for her to come over. She could just be greeting us though.

"So you're Emily's dad?" she asks. "Yes, I'm this angel's dad," Jess says looking at Emily. It's really none of her business tho.

"Are you single?" she asks batting her eyelashes. "You okay? If you keep batting your eyelashes they might just fly away," I tell her. She rolls her eyes at me and focuses back on Jess. "I'm not single, but in a relationship with this amazing woman right here," He says looking at me.

I wanna know what she'll do after that. If she'll be desperate enough to still try and get into his pants. "You're not married right?" she asks looking at him intently.

"I'm not married but you still won't have a chance," he said in an irritated tone. "You ready, love?" he asks me now ignoring her.

"Yup, let's go," I say holding his hand.

"Let's watch a movie," I suggest to Jess and Emily. "Ooo, mommy can we watch a funny movie?" Em asks.

"Uh, sure baby," I say. I look at Jess asking if he wants to join and he says sure.

I pick up Emily, carrying her on my hips and walked to the living room with Jess following closely behind. I placed her on the couch gently and sat beside her while Jess grabbed the remote.

We skipped through Netflix going through a bunch of different movies and shows. Minutes later all 3 of us came to an agreement on Mall Cop.

20 minutes into the movie I went to the kitchen to get candies like gummy worms & bears, sour patch kids, skittles, Snickers and a big bag of Doritos for us to share. I also got some drinks for us.

Emily fell asleep not too long ago and Jess decided it was time to make his "move" on me. I turned around to tell him something and he crashed his lips against mine, taking me by surprise.

"Em is already asleep, let's just put her in bed and head to bed," I tell him as I pull away from his now swollen pink lips.

I pick up Emily and walked to her room, Jess hot on my trail. I placed her in bed and then kissed her forehead. Jess also kissed her on the forehead and we left her room.

"Did you turn off the tv?" I asked Jess. "Yup," he said looking at me intently. I sit on the bed and Jess immediately sits beside me. He straddles me, hovering above my body. He gently kisses me, slowly and passionately. I tug at his shirt taking it off and he takes off mine.

We pause the kissing as we finished undressing and we are left in our birthday suits. He starts kissing my neck leaving hot tingles glistening on my skin. He goes agonizingly slow down my body, making me become frustrated and growing impatient.

He senses this and laughs at me. His strong laugh vibrations ripple through my body. I groan at him in irritation before flipping us over so he's under me.

I let my hands run down his body then I grab his man downstairs. I'm going to tease him so he knows how I felt. I smirk when he gasps at my touch. "You're gonna wish you didn't tease me, Mr Cole," I say in a low, sweet voice, a daring smile gracing my lips.

Chapter 23

3rd Pov

Jess woke Crystal up by peppering light kisses all over her body. Soon enough she began to wake, feeling the tingling sensations of his kisses. She smiled while stretching her arms enjoying their little moment.

"It's time to wake up, my love," he says looking at her adoringly. His eyes shone with happiness. He felt complete as he was living with 2 of the most important people in his life. Of course, he loves his daughter but is he in love with his daughter's mother, his girlfriend?

Yes, he's completely head over heels for the amazing woman who is lying beside him. All that is left is to utter those 3 words to her. He had been thinking about their relationship the past week and decides to make the 1st move in shifting their relationship to the next stage.

When she lays there, with her eyes closed, Jess begins to tickle her. She rolls over laughing as he continues to tickle her. "Okay, okay, stop," she says between laughs.

Crystal tries getting out of his hold but his grip is too strong. "Okay, I'm up," she says out of breath. He finally lets her go and she sits on the bed. "I'm going to kill you," Crystal tells him, playfully glaring at him.

"Which one do you like, baby girl?" Crystal asks Emily. "Ah, mommy, I like tha one with tha pwink pants and unicowrn shirt," she says pointing at it. "Okay baby, let's get you dressed then," Crystal says.

Crystal pulls Emily's hair into 2 large buns after getting her dressed. "You look gorgeous, my baby," Crystal says, kissing her forehead. "Thawnk you mommy," Emily says. Crystal then lifts Emily into her arms and carries her to the living room where Jess is.

Jess is wearing black jeans and a white Gucci shirt with his white shoes. Crystal leaves Emily with her dad and then heads to the room to get dressed.

She opens the closet and the 1st thing that catches her eyes is a pair of black leather pants. She grabs it and places it on the bed then goes back to the closet. She looks for her black bodysuit that has lace detailing on it, to pair with the black leather pants. She decides to pair them with her black leather boots.

She then sits by the mirror and does a neutral, natural makeup look with brown eyeshadows and a nude lip with a black liner. To complete her look she adds 2 necklaces and more rings to her fingers. She gives herself a once over in the mirror and nods her head, liking how she looks.

She then grabs her black Gucci purse to match her outfit and leaves the room. She goes to the living room where her family is waiting on her. "Love, you look absolutely beautiful," Jess says, staring at her. "Thank you, you look handsome yourself," she replies.

Jess parks the car outside his mom's mansion where the barbeque is being held. "You ready?" Jess asks Crystal. "Sure let's go," she replies. She has met Jess's friends and his mom before but she was still a little nervous. She gets quiet around relatively large groups of people she doesn't know too well.

Jess hops out of the car and goes to Crystal's side to open the door for her. He offers her his hand and she takes it. She gets out of the car and Jess opens Emily's door and takes her out.

They walk up to the door and Jess rings the doorbell. They wait about 30 seconds before Jess's mom opens the door. "Hello son, Crystal and my beautiful grandbaby," Jess's mother says greeting them with a smile on her face.

"Hi mom," Jess says, kissing her cheek. "Hi Miss Gyanor," Crystal says, giving her a smile. "Dear call me mom or Shayan," She says, giving her a warm smile. Crystal nods in response, not really knowing what to say. She hasn't seen her own family in years.

"Hi grawndma," Emily says, giving Shayan a big smile. "Let's go inside, shall we?" Shayan says smiling.

"Everyone's in the backyard," Shayan says. "You guys go, I'll go in the kitchen to get some stuff," she added. Jess takes Crystal's hand and guided her to the backyard.

"Hey everyone," Jess says, announcing his presence. They all turn their attention to him. They all replay with choruses of heys and hi's.

"Hi," Crystal says waving at them. She's only met some of the people here. Which was when they ran into each other at the bar. Jess guides Crystal and Emily over to 2 of his friends.

"They are Kira and Mace," Jess says, gesturing to the 2 adults. "And these 3 cuties are Jake, Ira, and Zeke," jess says, referring to the 3 children that sat near them on a blanket.

"They are Crystal and my daughter Emily," Jess tells Mace and Kira, pointing at Crystal and Emily. "Hey guys," Crystal says. "I Aunty Kira and Uncle Mace," Emily says smiling at them. "Mommy, can I play with Jake and Ira, please?" Emily asks.

"Of course, baby," Crystal says and Emily sits on the blanket with them. "Your kids are so beautiful," Crystal tells them. "Thank you," both Kira and Mace respond. "Can I hold Zeke, I just love babies," Crystal asks. "Sure, let me give you some hand-sanitiser first," Kira says, digging in her purse. Kira gives Crystal some hand sanitiser then hands over Zeke to her.

After Jess, Crystal, Kira and mace talked, Jess introduced his girls to the rest of the people. They ate, talked, played board games and watched a movie.

Crystal had gotten along with everyone and had a great time together.

Chapter 24

C   r   y   s   -
tal

Jess and I are going on a date tonight. Right now I'm getting ready to go shopping with Jayla and Emily. I have already gotten Em ready.

Soon enough I found an outfit, I chose a burgundy sweatshirt and paired it with white pants and sneakers. I grabbed my white purse-bag, and then packed it with both things for me and Emily.

Jess has already gone to work, he also won't tell me what were doing for the date. I picked up Emily from the bed, then trudged down the stairs with her in my arms. I then went to the front door and grabbed my keys that sat on the little table by the door.

>>>>>>>>>>>

I had met Jayla in the mall's parking lot then we headed through the doors, entering the busy mall.

"Where should we go 1st?" Jayla asked as she surveyed the mall.

"Ummmm.... How about Darling Ash?" I asked. I was glad I had brought Em's stroller with me or else I would be struggling. She was good as long as she wasn't hungry and she had some sort of entertainment which was where her Ipad handily came in.

"Sure, they have nice jewellery," she says, smiling brightly at the idea of jewellery. We walk over to the store hand in hand. "Ooo, lwok at all the pwetty clothes," Emily says as her eyes wander over the different things.

We laugh lowly at her fondness. "I don't know what to wear, he told me nothing about what we're doing," I softly groan in frustration. "Crysie, don't stress, he told me the basics of your date so I could make sure your fat ass is not stressing," Jayla says, rubbing my shoulders. I roll my eyes and softly push her away.

"Awesome, I can go kick my feet up and drink cham-pagne while you go find me a jaw-dropping outfit for tonight," I say sarcastically.

She takes Emily's stroller out of my hands and begins to push it along, looking through different items. I lag behind them. "Come on C, we don't have all day," Jayla says. I don't respond but catch up. "We should've gotten coffee, I need energy," I say lowly.

>>>>>>>>>>>>>

We went to 2 more stories after Darling Ash, now we are walking through the doors of the 4th store of today. Walking into the store my eyes caught on a mustard, bright yellow jumper dress. I walked over to it quickly, taking it from the rack.

I looked over to Jayla to see she was already looking at me. "Can I wear it?" I say voicing my thoughts. "You would look so good in that," Jayla says.

>>>>>>>>>>

"You look beautiful, love," Jess tells me as I step off the last step of the stairs. "Thank you, baby, you look handsome," I say as I walk toward him.

"You guys enjoy your date," Jayla says winking at us. "Take good care of our baby, Jayla," Jess says. Jayla simply smiles in response.

"Okay go you guys, I have everything handled," Jayla says as she pushed Jess and me out the door. "Okay, bye baby girl," I say kissing Em's forehead. Jess does the same and we head off.

>>>>>>>>>>>>

Jess had taken me to a cute cottage restaurant. The workers were respectful as we could see so far and the place looked stunning. The restaurant had plants almost everywhere and it had other cute floral detail. It gave off an outdoor indoor vibe and it also had a little water fountain with a mermaid as its design.

"What would you like to order, sir, miss?" A waiter asked coming up to our table. Jess nodded at me, saying I should order first. "I would like a grill cheese sandwich with fries and a bottle of Sprite, please," I tell the waiter. "I'd like the classic burger, cheese fries with water, please," Jess orders.

The waiter give us a polite nod followed by an okay then went on his way. Jess and I then began to talk. Having conversations about any and everything, getting to know each other better and so on.

>>>>>>>>>>>

3rd pov

"Can we go to the park, Aunty Lala?" Emily asked Jayla. Jayla stayed silent for a moment, thinking before she answered. "Sure baby, I don't see why not," she said.

"Go get your backpack and we'll leave in 20 minutes," Jayla said. Emily got down off of the couch, then went to her room to get her bag. Jayla then turned her attention back to the show they were watching.

>>>>>>>>>>>>>

"How about the slide, sweetheart," Jayla asked Emily. Emily nodded eagerly as she was excited to go on the slide.

Jayla had a smile playing on her lips as she watched the little girl going down the big, bright blue slide. Sure, Emily wasn't hers but she had been with her when she was in her mom's room and she loves that little girl to death.

"Can you push me on the swing, please," Emily says as she sits beside Her aunty on the bench? "Sure baby, let's go," Jayla says as she gets up.

"Weee!" Emily says as Jayla pushes her. "Hold on ting, Em," Jayla says as she pushes her again. Emily kicks her short little legs in the air.

"You tired, baby," Jayla asks Emily. "Yes aunty," she says. "Let's go sit on the benches, you can eat your snack then," Jayla says. Jayla picks up Em, settling her on her hips then she walks over to the closest empty bench.

Jayla sits on the bench placing Emily on her lap then putting her backpack beside them. "Let me get your snack and juice for you, sweetheart," Jayla says as she opens Emily's bag.

A couple of minutes later a woman walks over to Jayla and Emily.

Realizing someone is in front of her Jayla looks up, "may I help you?" Jayla asks politely. "No, not really," she says before plopping down beside them.

Jayla had an eerie feeling about the woman but shook it off. It didn't take long for the woman to begin to talk. Jayla was not too keen on the woman but the be polite she indulged in the woman's conversation.

Emily was still in Jayla's lap, she was sleeping, so the women keep their voices at a reasonable level. Jayla turned her head a little to reach for something in her purse. As soon as she turned she felt a sharp prick in her neck. She turned around swiftly only to see the woman holding a syringe.

Jayla tried to get up but she felt droopy, whatever drugs the woman injected into her were starting to take effect. The woman picked up Emily and her bag and then walked away leaving an unconscious Jayla on the bench.

>>>>>>>>>>>>

Emily opened her eyes seeing she was in an unfamiliar car. She shook her head, shaking off the sleep. She blinked a couple of times trying to herself to focus.

Emily then realized the person drive g the car was the woman from the park. She was confused as to where Jayla was and voiced her question.

"Where is my aunty?" Emily asked. The woman couldn't turn around as she was driving so she glanced in the rearview mirror. "I left your aunty at the park," the woman said cooly.

"Who are you and Why am I with you?" Emily asked oddly calm. "My name is Jessica, and I'm kidnapping you because I want your father and he's with your whore of a mother," the woman told the child bitterly.

Emily didn't understand the meaning of the word whore but she assumed it meant something negative based on the facial expression the woman showed when she said it.

"Okay," Emily says as she looked out the window. She knew her mother would do her best to find her and she wasn't too worried, she just hoped the crazy woman in the driver's seat didn't do anything bad to her aunt.

The woman found the child odd as she was being kidnapped but wasn't crying for her parents nor making any noise. It's like the little girl understood to an extent what was happening. She had never seen a child that behaved as this one did.

Jessica is in love with Jess and will do anything to have him. Jessica is Jess's ex-secretary and when she found out about Crystal and them having a child together she went ballistic.

>>>>>>>>>>>>>

Jessica pulled into the driveway of an old abandoned house. She parked the car before opening the door and grabbing Emily from the backseat.

Emily stayed quiet as she observed her surroundings and the woman who had kidnapped her.

"Are you broken?" Jessica asked Emily as she sat in front of her. "Nope, how long will I be here, before the cops come to get you," Emily asked her. Jessica was taken aback by the little girl's question. She couldn't have been more than 6 years of age, the woman thought.

"I have a question for you," Emily tells the woman. Jessica nodded her head. She didn't really want to deal with the child but she would somewhat entertain it. "If you hate my mother, why isn't she the one you kidnapped," Emily said.

Emily found the woman dumb. All though she knows her dad loves her, she isn't the love of his life but her mother.

The woman was speechless. "I don't know," Jessica responded to the child. "You're dumb," the child stated. "You know I can hurt you right?" Jessica asks the child feeling offended.

>>>>>>>>>>>>>>

"Hello," Crystal says as she answers the phone. "Yes, um... is the Crystal Myers?" the voice asks. "Yes, this is she," Crystal says. "This is St. Jude's hospital and you are an emergency contact for Jayla Thrasher," the person says. "What has happened to her," Crystal says, worry etched in her tone. "She has been found unconscious in the park," the person says. "Before I hang up, is there a little girl with her?" Crystal asks the person. "No ma'am,"

The person says.

At the person's words, her heart dropped. She frantically explained the situation to Jess before they paid and left.

Crystal was very worried, her best friend was in the hospital and her daughter could not be found. Jess was beside her in the car and on the phone with the police.

Jess was very worried about his daughter. He was scared for Jayla, yes, but his daughter was missing and probably have been kidnapped. The couple was distressed.

>>>>>>>>>>>>>

The police had met with jess and Crystal at the hospital. Crystal was glad to know Jayla wasn't seriously hurt and that she would wake up in a couple of hours.

They discussed how to find Emily. Suddenly Crystal remembered that there was a tracker in the special necklace she gave Emily. She had quickly taken out her phone, searching for the app.

"I know where Emily is," Crystal says showing them her phone screen. "Thank God, I had put that in her necklace as a safety feature," she says. She let out a deep breath somewhat happy that the situation was getting better. The couple hoped whoever had taken their daughter didn't do anything to her.

>>>>>>>>>>>>>>>>>

Emily smiled as she saw the flashing lights of the police outside. "Come outside, we have you surrounded," a voice boomed.

Jessica began to panic. How had they found her? She asked herself. She gave up, she had gotten caught. She wasn't even sure what she was even going to do to the child anyway.

She slowly walked outside. The police quickly cuffed her and barged into the abandoned house in search of the little girl.

They took her outside and she looked around to see if her parent were there. Her mom ran to her pulling her in her arms. Jess was close behind.

"Baby, are you okay?" Jess asked Emily. "I'm fine daddy, the crazy woman didn't do anything," Emily said hugging her dad back. "She's obsessed with you though," Emily added.

Chapter 25

Jess

"Shall we take a walk on the beach, I got you slippers?"
I ask. "Yup," she says linking her arms with mine.

"Did you get it?" I ask into my phone. I was talking to
one of my best friends, Kyle. "Yeah man, it's great, you
sure about this?" He asks. "Yup, of course, I am, I love
her," I answer before hanging up.

I walk out of the bathroom and then went down to the
kitchen. I walked up to Emily and placed a kiss on her
forehead. "Good morning, princess," I say. "Morning,
daddy," she says as she takes a sip of orange juice from
her Cinderella cup.

Crystal was at the stove making scrabble eggs and I
walked over to her. I then wrapped my arms around her

waist and kissed her neck. "Good morning, beautiful," I say, giving her a smile. "Good morning baby," she says.

She spins around, turning towards me and wraps her arms around my neck. She then leans into me and plants a chaste kiss on my lips. I pull her closer and deepened the kiss. Seconds later she pulls away. "Go sit beside Em (Emily), I'll finish cooking," she says and gives me one last kiss before turning me in Ems's direction.

"Oh, babe, I'm taking you out later," I tell her. Don't worry about Emily my mom is babysitting, I add.

>>>>>>>>>>>>>

After breakfast, I went out to get things in preparation for later on today. I just hope she says yes. I hired a few people to help me with this as well as some of my friends.

I've been jittery thinking about this all week and to be honest I'm very nervous.

I park my car in the lot of this famous flowers store. I grab my phone out of my centre console and get out.

There was a house illuminated sign with Delight Florals It had different flowers and plants on it too.

I opened the door to the store and is greeted by beautiful floral arrangements. "May I help you with something?" A store worker asks.

"Ah yes, What would be the best flowers to give to the love of your life?" I ask the worker. "I would say carnations," the worker replies.

"Could you show me some, please?" I ask politely. "Sure Sir, follow me," she says before walking away.

She brings me over to a relatively long table with all types of carnations. "I'll have a bouquet with the red, white and pink ones, please," I say.

"Sure, you can take a seat over there while you wait," she says.

About 15 minutes later I was able to walk out with a bouquet of carnations. Now it's time to go home to the love of my life and my amazing daughter.

>>>>>>>>>>>>

I see Em in the living room, watching Paw patrol. I walk over to her and kiss her on the head before going to find Crystal.

"Are you getting ready?" I call out as I enter our bedroom. I didn't give her a specific time that we would leave so I wasn't surprised if she was getting ready now. "In here," I hear her soft voice calling out. She was in the bathroom so I walked over. "I'm coming in, love," I say before opening the door.

My dick immediately hardened at what I walked in on. Crystal's leg was up on the white marble counter, she was naked and her beautiful long hair flowing down her back. She was lotioning her legs. "Do you need help with lotioning, because believe me I would be happy to," I tell her, my voice seeming to have gotten deeper.

"I'm all good, baby," she says winking at me.

I looked at my watch to see what time it was and its 4 pm, we have time.

* Spicy Content *

I walked over to her and smashed my lips on her plump, pink ones. She wrapped her hands around my neck as I bit her lower lip asking for entrance and she opened her mouth complying.

We stopped our tonsil wrestling to get breaths of hair. Her eyes were now hooded, shining with lust. I picked her up and she wrapped her legs around my torso. She then placed her hands on my face and held it while she kissed down my neck.

"You have on too many clothes, we need to change that," she smirks before coming out of my hands and then she began to unbutton my shirt.

After tossing my shirt somewhere in the bathroom she unblocked my belt and unbuttoned my pants, I helped her to get it off my body and she too discarded it.

We began kissing again but this time we were going to the bedroom. Seconds later I had her under me on our bed.

"Aren't we going out soon?" She asks breathlessly as I thrust into her. "Love, we have time," I say as I kiss down her neck.

She lets out a breathy moan as I bit her nipple, I then licked it and began to kiss around her supple breasts.

"Jess," she moans my name as she arches her back.

"Go faster," she says barely above a whisper. And I do just that. I can feel her getting close to the edge and my lips find hers.

I lift up her leg and hook it around me and I thrust into her harder. She cums as she screams out in ecstasy. Seconds later I released into her.

"You good, baby?" I ask as she lays still breathy heavily and her hair everywhere. I guess I did good and a grin spreads across my face.

"Shut up," she says rolling her eyes at me. "I loved it when you were rolling your eyes as I was fucking you," I smirk at her. This gets her to look at me. "I mean, I wouldn't mind doing that again," she says as her eyes run down my naked body. She's teasing me. "Round 2?" I ask.

"I have to get ready," she says as she walks into the bathroom.

I smile as I hear the door lock. I have to get ready too.

I go to the closet to pick out my clothes. I chose a black button-up shirt, black pants, black dress shoes and a black and white coat.

I go wait on the bed for Crystal to finish with the bathroom. I know I could just use a guest bathroom but I couldn't bother.

Luckily, I didn't have to wait long as five minutes later she comes out with her silk black robe draped around her body.

....
Crystal is wearing a skin-tight red dress with matching red heels and gold jewellery adorns her sinfully beauti-ful body.

"You look stunning, love," I tell her as I kiss her Jaw. "Thank you, baby, you look edible," she says and gives me a wink. I give her a grin and held her hand then walked her to my car.

I hadn't given her the bouquet yet, so I quickly do that. They look beautiful, she says as her eyes scan the flowers. She smiles and thanks me giving me a quick peck. "What kind are they?" she asks curiously. "They're called carnations and they mean love, speaking of that I love you," I say.

"And I love you, she says," a soft smile gracing her face.

"Ready, my love?" I ask her. "Yes, I am, darling," she responds. I open the passenger door and help her in. I close her door then walked over to my side and got in.

>>>>>>>>>>>>

We pulled into the parking lot of the private beach I rented for the night. I had bought her slippers for the sand so she wouldn't have to walk in heels for later when we are walking on the beach. I grab the bag with them from the back then go to open her door and gave her my hand, helping her out of the car.

"Okay, love, I have a dinner planned and then we have the beach to ourselves after," I tell her as I walk her in the direction of the private space. It's not a restaurant. I got chefs to make our favourite food, then I got a server to give it to us.

I walk her up the stairs to the platform. It had canopies, flower arrangements, and fairy lights and it was well decorated.

I pull out a chair for her and then seat her, I then go over to my side and sit down.

"Do you like it?" I asked her. "Yes, Jess, It looks gorgeous, thank you," she says, a beautiful smile on her beautiful face.

The server then came with the food, we thanked them and then they headed off.

Me and Crystal then fell into easy conversation while eating the food.

We just finished eating and were having light conversation.

I got up and pulled out the small black box out of my pocket. I got on one knee in front of her and showed her the ring. "Crystal Myers, the love of my life, mother of my child, most beautiful woman I've ever had the pleasure of meeting, will you make me the happiest man to ever live and marry me?" I ask.

At this point, silent tears were streaming down her face. "Yes, Yes I will," she says smiling brightly at me.

I stand up and kiss her passionately. "I love you," she says as she pulls away. "And I love you, always," I say.

Chapter 26

C   r   y   s   -
tal

"Hey baby," jess says kissing my forehead. "What's up," I say wrapping my arms around his waist. "I want you to hang out with my friends today," he says looking into my eyes somewhat pleadingly. "Please," he adds.

"Alright," I say. I placed a delicate kiss on his lips then moved away from him and continued to put away things, cleaning up our currently messy kitchen.

"What about Emily?" I asked. Today was my day off, Jayla was at the hospital, she has maybe a 15-hour shift today, and although she loves Emily, I don't want to always ask her to babysit her.

"Well we are meeting them after 3, so Emily will be out, there will be 3 nannies there to help with the kids," he says.

"Okay then, where are we going?" I asked now looking at him. "We're going to this Mexican restaurant and it has an arcade nearby where we'll go after lunch." He says. "Alright babe, wanna help me pick out an outfit," I say, walking towards the stairs. "Yes, love," he says and begins to walk towards me.

>>>>>>>>>>>>

"Should I go with leather pants?" I asked holding said pants up "Hmmm," he hums. "What shirt would you wear with it though?" He asks. "Maybe an oversized sweatshirt," I tell him.

I met his friends like 3 times before and they seem nice enough, can't really judge since I don't really know them, but I hope today will be fun.

"Wait... we are going to get lunch first, right?" I ask, even though I knew the answer already. "Yup," He says.

I deadfall on the bed letting out a sigh. "You are no help," I said, poking him in his side. He rolls his eyes at me," Darling, I am the most fashionable person ever."

"You pick it then," I say, lightly punching his arm. "Alright, fine, crazy woman," he mumbles loud enough for me to hear. I punch him again. He holds his hands up in surrender and jumps off the bed.

He disappears into our closet and comebacks about 10 minutes later holding 3 outfits. "Outfit number one," he says, holding up a red breezy, frilly dress with lace embellishments.

"Outfit number 2," he says, showing me the red leather skirt and oversized black. "Outfit number 3," he says, holding up the black, grey and white plaid pants and the plain white button-up shirt.

"Which one do you fancy, love," he says as he sits beside me. "What are you wearing?" I ask him. I'm thinking of choosing outfit number 3, I kind of want us to match.

"Not sure yet? He says. "I'm choosing outfit 3," I say. "You want to match?" He asks smiling at me. "Yes," I say, sounding a bit excited and he laughs at me.

\>>>>>>>>>>>>>

"Jess, It's time to go pick up Emily!" I shout from the living room as he's in his office. "Okay, love!" he yells back.

Jess will go pick up our daughter while I get her clothes and stuff together. I pick out some pink leggings and a pink and white shirt that says 'I'm a star' with a purple star with a smiley face.

\>>>>>>>>>>>>>>

We walked through the doors of the Mexican restaurant. It's called Tan Deliciouso. "Table under Regan, please," Jess tells the lady at the reception desk. "Okay sir, follow me," she says and leads us to the table.

She takes us to a somewhat private, secluded area of the restaurant where a huge table is located. Kira and Mace are there and they have their 3 kids; Jake, Ira and Zeke with them.

Emily immediately lets go of my hands and goes over to Jake and Ira. They begin to talk and wander off in their own little bubble. Kira has Zeke and I go talk with her. We fall into easy conversation while Mace and Jess do a bro-hug and begin to talk to each other.

A couple of minutes later the whole gang has arrived but Kyle. "Should we order now, guys?" Scarlet asks. Mumbles of yeses from the rest of us were what she got in response.

"Waiter," she says, flagging down the server closest to her. "Good afternoon everyone, what may I get you all?" he asks politely.

"I'll have the Sopes and tortillas, please," Scarlett says, looking at her menu. Kyle then walks in and he has a woman with him. She has light brown hair, that flows down her shoulders and brown eyes.

"Sorry I'm late guys," he says. "This is my friend Mari-ah," he adds, sitting down. We all greet them and get back to ordering our food. I order Emily chimichangas, they aren't too flavourful, spicy or anything like that so I think it'll be fine for her.

Jess got tacos and a soup called 'Sopa de Fideo'. I went with Carne Asada and Tortas. As we waited for our food conversation began to flow around the table.

"So Mariah, how do you know kyle?" Kira asked Mariah. The table became quiet listening to Kira asking Mariah things. "We are friends from college," she says.

"I've never known Kyle having female friends apart from us, ya'll fucking? Scarlett asks her. Mariah's face reddens a bit before answering no. "Scarlet, behave!" Ray said. "I didn't say it to be rude," she mumbles but we can still hear her.

A Few minutes after that our food came and we dug in but the conversations were still alive. A couple of times I noticed Mariah staring a Jess. It was the dreamy stare too. I know he's handsome and all that but does he seriously have to have such an effect on the female species.

"Jess, right?" she asks. Her elbows rest on the table, her hands holding her face she's in a kind of bending position.

I'm slightly turned to Kira, whom I'm having a talk with but I'm hyper-aware of their little conversation and I raise my right eyebrow. I know where this is going and it seems Kira can too.

"Yes," Jess answers trying to sound polite. "So, you're friends with everyone here?" she asks. "yup, known them since we were kids," he says.

"Do you have a girlfriend?" she asks twirling a piece of her hair. I wasn't going to say anything or do anything, I want to see where this goes, not yet at least.

Jess stays quiet and holds my left hand up to her face, showing her my ring. At this point, I turn around in their direction as she's sitting on the other side of him next to Kyle.

"Oh," she says a little disappointed. Everyone else's conversations have toned down listening to what's go-ing on with amused faces. "Girl, I don't know how you're so calm right now," Kiras says to me and I shrug in response.

"Engaged or married," she asks a somewhat hopeful look in her eyes. Before jess can answer Emily goes to

Jess," Daddy, can I borrow your phone, please?" she asks. "Sure baby girl," he says. He then gives her the phone and Emily goes back to playing with Jake and Ira.

Mariah's eyes widened at Emily and the hope in her eyes disappears. "Engaged and hopefully married soon," he says smiling at me and I smile at him back.

Jess then leans over and kisses me lightly on the lips and goes back to eating his food ignoring Mariah.

I feel eyes on me and I look up to see Mariah glaring at me. I give her a bored look and then help Kira with Zeke. "Crystal, Mariah was definitely glaring at you," Scarlett says. Kira hums in agreement. " I can beat a bitch up if you want," Kira says. "No need to worry ladies, " I say laughing a little.

I'm happy they don't hate me and they have my back. "Thank you guys though, Jayla would love you guys," I say smiling at her. "How about we have a girls' day," Scarlette says. "And we could meet your best friend, maybe we can all become friends," Kira finishes.

>>>>>>>>>>>>

After dinner, we went to the arcade. It was a lot of fun. Emily definitely had a good time by the time we were home she was fast asleep.

"I'm surprised you weren't jealous today," Jess says as he lays in bed next to me. "I was, I just know how to hide it better than you," I say smirking at him. He laughs and pulls me closer to him.

"Scarlett and Kira were ready to rip her head off though," I tell him. "I know, they weren't quiet about it," he says.

"Let's go to bed I'm tired," I say. "Goodnight, love" Jess says kissing my forehead.

Chapter 27

Crystal

"I love you, I'm going to work now, bye baby," I say as I plant a kiss on Jess's forehead. He was still in bed sleeping and I didn't want to wake him up. It was quite early. I had already gotten Emily ready for school and I'll drop her off before going to work.

>>>>>>>>>>>>

"Goodbye, my baby, I love you, have a wonderful day, your dad will pick you up later," I say as I walk Emily to her school's entry. I kiss her cheek and then watch her walk through the doors before leaving.

>>>>>>>>>>>>>

"Good morning Elena," I say, walking past her desk. "Morning, Crystal," she says, giving me one of her bright smiles. She's such a cheery person.

"Hello Mr Ellsion, are you ready for your check-up?" I ask the old man. He's been my patient for a while now and he's been wonderful. He has diabetes and he only has his granddaughter left. Poor souls, they are. "Wonderfull to see you, Doctor Myers," he says politely. "How's Lacy?" I ask as I take his blood pressure. "She's been good, she recently got a new job," he says. "That's great," I told him, giving him a polite smile.

I like making small talk with my patients, it helps settle their nerves and not make it so awkward. "Your pressure is good, have you been following the diet I put you on?" I ask him. "Yes ma'am," he says, mocking me. I laugh at his antics as I check his heartbeat.

"You're engaged now," he states. I look at him seeing him stare at the ring on my finger. "I am," I say. "Congratulations, you're a very nice lady," he says. "Thank you, Mr Ellison," I say, giving him a gentle smile. "Okay, you're good," I say as I finish up with him.

>>>>>>>>>>>>>>>

It's my lunchtime and Jayla and I are going to check out this new cafe. It's about 15 minutes from where we are.

We reach there and the front is green and a creme colour. Walking into the cafe it has an earthy vibe. We find a table and sit as well as look at the decor. It has a very natural, earthy aesthetic.

Jayla and I begin to catch up as we've both been quite busy this past week. "I got a boyfriend," Jayla suddenly blurts out. I look at her before a grin graces my face. "That's great, honey, are you happy with him?" I ask her. Jayla is amazing and she deserves the world. This man better be good to her. "Guess who's engaged," I say as I bite my lip.

Her eyes widen and she stares at me. I hold up my hand to her face and she squeals excitedly. "Oh my gosh, Crystal!" she whisper-shouts. "I'm so happy for you bestie," she says, giving me a big smile.

"It's good that you found love, you've struggled way too much not to end up happy," she says. She then gets up and hugs me. "If you don't let go I might die," I tell her, pulling away from her tight hug. She lightly hits my shoulder and returns to her seat.

We talked some more before the waitress came to take our order. I ordered matcha tea and Jayla ordered a Chai latte.

A little while later the door to the cafe opens and I turn to look at who entered. Why? Because of human curiosity...

The light shone in my eyes so it took a while for me to see the person but I could make out that the person was a male. There was also someone else behind them. They walked further into the room and that is when I could fully see the person's face. Confusion clouded my mind as I saw that the man was looking at me. I turned around and then continued my conversation with Jayla.

A few minutes later I checked my watch and realized I had to leave to go back to work. Jayla and I hug before I leave. As I Was leaving I realized the man and woman from earlier were sitting at the table behind me.

Passing by them I noticed him looking at me intent-ly. He had reddish auburn hair and hazel eyes which pierced through me. He was attractive, not gonna lie but I only have eyes for Jess and I got a bad feeling about Hazel eyes.

>>>>>>>>>>>>>

~ A week later ~

My shift was about to end and Jess is picking me up today since my Audi is being serviced. I got a text from Jess saying he was outside and I told him that I'm on my way.

I grabbed my bag from the locker and shut it then headed out of the building. As I opened the door some-one grabbed me and pinned me to the wall. "What the-," I say, my words trailing off as I realized it was the cafe dude, Hazel eyes, from a week ago.

"Let me go," I told him sternly. "No my beautiful lady, give me a chance," he said staring intently at me. "No, I'm engaged and leave me alone you creep!" I almost shout. He makes a "tsk" sound and grips my wrist tightly. I try pulling away from him but it doesn't work so I kick him where the sun definitely doesn't shine.

I quickly run away when he kneels on the ground holding his crotch area. "You bitch!" I heard him shout as I was leaving. I look around the parking lot for Jess's car and I let out a deep breath when I finally found it.

I opened the door and sat in the passenger seat. I sigh and rub my eyelids, a frown took over my face. "Are you okay, luv," Jess asks, his face showing worry. "I think so," I respond after a short pause of silence.

"Did something happen, darling?" he asks holding my hands. I let out a sigh and decided to tell him what happened. "So, when I was coming out and dude pinned me against the wall, the funny thing is I saw him a week ago in a cafe and he was staring at me creepily," I tell him.

Anger flashed in his eyes as he soaked in what I just told him. "Did he say anything to you?" he asked. "He told me to give him a chance, he was basically trying to get me," I said. I rubbed my wrist, it still burned a little from Hazel eye's tight grip.

"Did the bastard hurt you?" he said rubbing patterns on my hand. I think he's trying to calm himself down and not rip off Hazel eye's head, I mean I wouldn't mind that.

"He just grabbed my wrist tightly, and didn't want to let go, I had to kick him in the balls," I told him. "Do you think he's stalking you, my love?" He asks. "Probably, because how would he know where I work and that I would be there," I say.

 "Can we go home I'm tired," I say leaning back in my seat. "Yes, baby, but we will be talking about this later," he tells me.

Chapter 28

3rd Pov

Crystal, Jayla, Emily, Kira, Scarlet and Ira walked into the infamous 'Forever A Bride' wedding shop. The store was mostly white with beautiful dresses and other accessories displayed aesthetically.

"May I help you beautiful ladies, today?" A lady asked, politely.

"Hello, and yes you may," Kira told the sweet lady. "I'm Lauren, which one of you ladies is the bride?" Lauren said as her eyes drifted over the women. "That would be me," Crystal spoke up. "Ah, wonderful. Do you have anything you have in mind?" Lauren asked Crystal.

"Not really, I just wanted to look at them to see if any of them, in particular, would wow me," Crystal said.

"Oh nothing with long sleeves though," Crystal added quickly, a slight grimace on her face.

"Follow me, ladies," Lauren said as she walked further into the store. "We will be also getting bridesmaids' dresses as well as dresses for these 2 cuties," Crystal told Lauren. "Of course," Lauren says. "Today's gonna be a long day," Jayla said and the group laughed.

"Let me go get some dresses to start off with," Lauren said then scurried off. "What colours are you and Jess using for the wedding, C?" "We agreed on peach and white," Crystal answered.

Crystal's Pov

"Okay, I have 4 dresses to start off us with," Lauren says as she displayed the dresses.

The 1st one was slim at the bottom like a mermaid dress and the top and a deep v neckline with puffy sleeves. The 2nd one I won't bother to describe as it was so atrocious looking. The 3rd one's top part was mostly all lace with off the shoulder puffy sleeves. It wasn't bad it gave me garden fairy vibes.

The 4th and final dress was short in the front and long in the back as well as it was pretty puffy. A huge no for me. Lauren took one look at my face, "None made the cut, did it?" she asked. I nodded my head with a grimace on my face.

"Can we just look around the shop?" Jayla asked. That bitch really read my mind. I nodded eagerly in compliance with Jayla. "Of course, let's go," Lauren says. She then walks off leaving us to follow behind her.

"How about this one?" Kira asked, holding up a black goth puffy dress. Scarlet burst out in a fit of laughter. "She's not the vampire queen like you Kira," Scarlet said as she sobered up. Kira rolled her eyes at her. "I agree with Scar Scar," Jayla says. "Scar Scar?" Scarlet inquired. "Girl, I'm too lazy to say Scarlet, plus Scar Scar is better," Jayla says grinning at her.

Scarlet shook her in amusement and a small smile graced her lips.

>>>>>>>>>>>>>

After an hour of looking at the wedding dresses, I finally found the perfect dress. It had a deep v neckline with a lace top, it had a slit then run up her leg and a mermaid tail like bottom with a small train.

"What do you guys think," I asked. "I think it totally your style," Jayla says looking at the dress. "Go try it on, C," Kira says. "Umm... Laura, where is the changing room?" Crystal asked. "Right there," She says pointing at it. "Do you need help?" Jayla asks. "Yup, thank you," I said giving her a smile.

"This is a whole hassle," I say Jokingly as Jayla zips up the dress. We've been trying to get it on for about 5 minutes. "We're done," she says, letting out a dramatic sigh. I shove her lightly laughing at her antics.

Jess

I heard my phone ding signifying that I had gotten a message. I quickly took out my phone, thinking it was Crystal. She went wedding dress shopping today. I wanted to see the dress but she said I had to wait until our wedding day.

My face opened with face ID and I went straight to messages but it wasn't Crystal who texted me it was an unknown number. It was a picture of Crystal in a wedding dress. It looked like those photos paparazzi would take of celebrities unknowingly. The person sent a text under it, "My bride looks so pretty, doesn't she?" It says. What the fuck do they mean their bride?

"Who the hell is this?" I texted back. I wait for a little while but received no response. I'm so pissed. That creep better not try anything with Crystal. I bet it's the dude that showed up at her workplace. I'll get one of my tech people to get his info.

I clicked on Crystal's contact. "What's up, baby?" Crystal asks. "You're stalker texted me something creepy. I need to get bodyguards for you and Emily, I'm not risking anything. Please let me do this," I say pleading. I will go absolutely crazy if anything happens to her or Emily.

She sighs before answering, "Okay Jess, we'll talk about this whole situation later." "Definitely, my love, I love you," I tell her. "I love you, bye," she says then hangs up.

"You okay, dude? Mace asks. "Crystal has a stalker and he's fucking psychotic," I tell him. "Well, shit," was his response. "So, what are you doing about it?" He inquires. "I'm getting her and Emily bodyguards, and I'm going to convince Crystal to take out a restraining order against him - I don't want that fucker near my family," I say.

I had already gotten my suit and my friends got their groomsmen suits as well. It wasn't a very long process. Also, Zeke, Mace and Kira's son, will be our ring bearer and of course, Em will be the flower's girl.

I can't wait to make Crystal my wife.

Chapter 29

J   e   s   s

Cole

I woke up with a smile on my face this morning. It doesn't feel like anything can ruin today for me. I have this weird feeling in my belly - it's somewhat a mixture of excitement, nervousness and happiness.

Emily comes running into Crystal and I's room, not wanting her to wake Crystal up, I bring her downstairs, and make breakfast.

"Today's a big day, sweetheart, you ready for it?" I ask her.

"Yes, daddy, I get to throw flowers everywhere!" she says animatedly, showing her small teeth in the process. "That's good, baby girl," I say smiling.

>>>>>>>>>>>>

"Hi, is everything going on track, I don't need any mishaps on my wedding day," I ask into the phone.

I'm talking to our wedding planner, her job is to make sure all the arrangements are good and nothing goes wrong.

"Yes, Mr Cole," She responds. "Okay, good," I tell her.

"Have you communicated with Mr Hasang, yet?" I ask. "Yes, he says that he'll scope out the venue and church before, as well as have guards watching every entry and exit," she responds.

"Okay, thank you, call me if there is any trouble that you cannot handle," I tell her. "Goodbye, Miss Lansen," I say before hanging up.

We will be getting at ready the hotel to save time and make it easier for us.

I have hired security to make sure that idiot doesn't mess with my wife or ruin our wedding day. I will not have that happening.

Crystal Myers

I'm having wedding jitters. "Crystal, calm down hun, everything will be fine," Jayla says as she strokes my back. I'm pretty sure she can see the nervousness on my face as clear as day.

"Where's Em?" I ask Kira as she walks through the door.

"Scar has her and the rest of the kids, they're buying snacks," she says.

"Are the hair and makeup people here yet?" she asks. "Nope, they'll be here soon though," Jayla responds.

Kira hums in response. She then goes and sits on the couch typing on her phone.

I assume she's texting her husband, Mace. I wonder if she's trying to get info on the men.

A few minutes later, I hear knocks on the door. "You guys are here now," I say opening the door. "Yup," Scarlet says as she hushers in the kids.

I got Emily dressed in her cute little peach and white dress, silver shoes and a pink headband with white flowers on it.

Kira also had gotten Ira into her clothes. She's in a fully peach dress with white adorable hearts adorning the dress.

She's also wearing a kawaii white headband with red and white flowers on it. They both look so angelic and beautiful.

>>>>>>>>>>>>>>

The hair and makeup entourage are here and they started a few seconds ago. We, women, collectively, got manicures and pedicures yesterday.

I got a cute French tip with medium length and a beautiful, vibrant peach polish for my toes. Jayla went with long peach nails and black French-tip for her toes.

Scarlet went for plain white medium length nails and red toes. And finally, Kira went for black everything. She's like a little goth queen and we tease her about it all the time.

The lady doing my hair, who I've come to know as Miriam, straightens my long, shiny black curly hair and puts it into an elegant updo with 2 mere strands of my here framing my face gently.

Miriam then goes on to do Jayla's hair and Kristen, the makeup lady comes over and gets started on my makeup.

Kristen did a neutral brown eyeshadow and silver on top of it. She also did one of the neatest wings I've ever seen someone do. And she did it so quickly too. I asked her what was her secret and she shrugged with a cheeky smile on her face. She added a bold red lip outlined with black and highlighter to my cheekbones.

After she had finished the ladies helped me put on the gown and heels.

After a while, we all were finished getting ready.

Jayla had a nude lip and silver eyeshadow with peach outlining it. Kira had on a pink gloss with light pink and nude eyeshadow. Scarlet has a brown nude base with gold outlining it.

All the ladies wore flowy peach dresses with a sweetheart neckline and lace fringe at the bottom and white heels. They all looked equally stunning.

Jess Cole

We all got ready fairly quickly. I'm wearing a white 3-piece suit with a peach tie and white shoes. I also added silver cufflinks to my suit sleeve.

Nate, Mace and Ray are wearing peaching suits with black ties and dress shoes. They look pretty dashing but I'll never admit it to them.

Especially, Nate, he's way too cocky. Don't need to inflate his already huge ego.

The boys, Jake and Zeke, are in full black tuxedos with black shoes. They look incredibly sharp and sleek. I want a son...

"Mr Cole, it's time to go to the alter," Miss Lansen says.

>>>>>>>>>>>>>

3rd Pov

They started to play the music then Emily walked along the aisle throwing the red and pink coloured roses out of the hand-crafted straw basket she had been given.

Then came along, Zeke, holding the clear plastic contraption that held the rings of the bride and groom. He walked along the aisle slowly and carefully not to trip and let the rings go flying.

Scarlet and Mace then go down the aisle hand in hand. Then the Regan couple walks and finally the maid of honour and best man, Jayla and Nate walk down the aisle.

Finally, Crystal, the stunning bride in white, begins to walk down the path that is the isle in the seemingly large church.

Her hands are covered with white gloves and a veil covers her pretty face. Pink and white coronation flowers made into an eye-catching bouquet in her hands.

A wide smile takes its place on Jess's face as he watches the love of his life walk towards him. In that moment, everything other than he and her, seems to fade into nothingness. His eyes become a bit more glassy with wetness as she nears him.

He looks at her in awe. "You look breathtaking, love," Jess whispers as Crystal stands before him.

"Thank you, baby, you look impeccable, my darling," she whispers back.

"Together we are gathered here for the union of Jess Cole and Crystal Myers," The pastor says.

"Do you, Jess Cole, take Crystal Myers, as your lawful wife, to have and hold, from this day forward, for better or for worse, for richer or for poorer, in sickness and in health, to love and cherish until death do you part?" The pastor asks.

"I do," Jess says, eagerly without hesitation.

"Do you, Crystal Myers, take Jess Cole, as your lawful husband, to have and hold, from this day forward, for better or for worse, for richer or for poorer, in sickness and in health, to love and cherish until death do you part?" The pastor asks her.

"I do," she says happily.

The pastor then turns to the crowd and asks, "If anyone objects to the marriage, speak now or forever hold your peace."

"I object!" says a man with intense hazel eyes among the sea of people. All heads snap to the man standing with his hand held in the air as if he was answering a question in school.

"Who the hell allowed this creep inside!" Jess asked rather loudly. The people looked back and forth between the two men with questioning looks on their faces.

Soon enough, the bodyguards came and dragged his sorry ass out of the church.

"Okay then, I now pronounce you husband and wife," the paster says looking somewhat confused.

"You may now kiss the-" Jess didn't wait for the pastor to say another word before he planted his lips on hers.

The people in attendance cheered happily with smiles on their faces.

They had thought the man was gone, but they were wrong. So very wrong...

The man ran back into the church hastily and pointed a gun at Jess and pressed down on the trigger, firing the bullet.

The people screamed as Crystal fell to the floor.

Jess looked at his now bloody bride on the floor clutching her side in horror. "Call an ambulance now!" I shouted as he bent down and held her in his arms.

"I guess the death part has come too quickly," The pastor says lowly. Jess turned his head and glared at the old, short balding man. The pastor held up his hands in surrender.

Agonizing minutes later, the ambulance came and hurried off with the bride. The groom was in the back of the ambulance holding on to his wife's hand for dear life.

Many depressing thoughts clouded his head as he prayed that she would die. Emily couldn't be left without her mother. And he couldn't bear to lose her, the love of his life.

Chapter 30

Crystal's Pov

It has been a month since I got out of the hospital. They kept me for a week after I woke up. Jess was a mess and Emily wasn't really aware of the situation.

Our wedding day was pretty much ruined by that idiot. I'm lucky I didn't die. Jess did tell me how stupid I was for taking the bullet for him but I didn't even think it just happened.

It took me forever to get Jess to agree on us going on the Hunny moon. I think we deserve one after what happened.

"Hey love, how are you feeling," Jess asked as he sat on the bed beside me. "Babe, I've been discharged for a month, I'm good, stop worrying," I tell him. "I'll never stop worrying about you and Em," he says as he pushes my hair out of my face.

I just smiled at him. He saw me get shot. He probably thought I was going to die - he's not going to get over it so easily.

I lean over and place a gentle but passionate kiss on his lips. I can feel him smile against my lips. I peck his lips quickly once more before moving away. "Are you sure your body can handle the honeymoon, love?" he asks.

"And I'm not talking about sex," he adds. "Did the doctor even give you the okay to do rigorous activities, I think not," he rants. I shake my head at him. "Baby, I feel fine, chill," I tell him. He huffs cutely and I laugh at him. He then frowns at me and playfully glares at me for laughing.

He lays down fully on our bed and I gently put his head on my lap. I then began to run my fingers through his soft, silky ash-blond hair. Why is his hair softer than mine?

He lets out a sigh, "that feels good." A smile slips on my face as I look down at him. "We are going on that honeymoon, I'm perfectly fine," I say firmly, leaving no room for argument. "Fine, you win, sweetheart," he says.

I give him a bright simile and he simply shakes his head at me.

>>>>>>>>>>>>>>>>>>>

"My mom wants to keep Em, that okay?" Jess asks. "Of course, babe," I say. "Oh, I bought the tickets, we're leaving in 4 days, on Tuesday afternoon," I inform him.

He nods, " Let's have a movie night," he suggests. "I'm down," I say. "Good, You go get Em, I'll set up and get the snacks," he tells me.

I walk up the stairs and then went to Emily's room. "Honey, your dad and I are having a movie night, you wanna join?" I ask her as I walk further into her room.

"Sure Mommy," she says. She then grabs her favourite baby blue bear which she named berry and her white blanket with sunflowers on them and then she stands in front of me and stretches her arms up in the air indicating that she wants me to carry her.

I scoop her petite body in my arms and then headed to the movie room.

"Okay, so what are we watching?" I ask. "How about this one Jess says clicking on some animated film called Sausage party. "Jess, that's rated R," I tell him. "Really? Oh shi-," he stops himself as Emily is in the room.

"Yeah, I'll take this," I say stretching over Em and taking the remote from him. I scroll down until I see Beverly Hill's Chihuahuas. "How about this?" I ask Jess. "It looks okay, Em, do you want to watch talking puppies?" He asks Emily.

"Puppies can't talk, daddy," she says sassily. "I know sweetheart but in the show, they have voice actors that play the characters," he explains to her.

"So do you wanna watch it, baby girl?" I ask her. "Okay mommy," she replies.

Jess

"Baby, you finish packing?" I ask entering our closet. She was bending down so she stood up, "yup," she says holding red g-strings between her fingertips.

I blink twice quickly before nodding my head in response. "I'll go put the suitcases in the car," I tell her. "Okay baby, I'm going to change though," She says.

I walk over to her and give her a quick kiss on the forehead. "Babe I just realized you bought tickets," I say. "Yeah and?" she questions. "I own a private jet, love," I say.

>>>>>>>>>>>>>>>>>>>

"If that flight attendant doesn't stop looking at you, I'm going to poke her eyes out," Crystal hissed from beside me. I laughed and patted her head while she glared at me. "We'll be landing soon, love, I think the plane ride is making you a bit grumpy," I told her.

She rolls her eyes and snuggles into my side more. "Wake me up when we're about to land, please," she says as she closes her eyes.

"It's so pretty," Crystal said animatedly. "It really is," I said standing beside her. No, I'm not being cliche like the movies and talking about her instead of the view. She's beautiful, gorgeous, not pretty.

"How about we get something to eat and then explore the hotel?" I ask. "Sure, sounds good," she says. She then stands on her tippy toes and stretches. The knots in her back make a cracking noise and she sighs.

"Let's shower and change before we do any of that though," she says and then drags me to the bathroom.

"We're showering together?" I ask her. "Yup," she responds. "Got a problem?" she adds as she begins to take off her shirt.

"No, no problem at all, love," I say, taking off my sweatpants.

Chapter 31

Jess Cole

Crystal giggles as I kiss down her torso. "Jess, we have to leave in 20 minutes," she says between breaths. "I know love," I reply before crashing my lips onto hers.

My tongue glides over her bottom lip. My hands go under the white flowy dress she has on and I gently squeeze her butt. I wait for her to take in a breath and then I sneak my tongue into her mouth.

Her tongue meets mine and our tongues begin to war for dominance. She grips the back of my head, pushing me more into her.

Eventually, she pulls away gasping for air. If we didn't need oxygen, our lips would still be glued together. I lick my swollen lips as I watch her exhale and inhale harshly.

She doesn't wait long before reconnecting our lips. "Baby, we've been making out for about 12 minutes, I think we should stop now," I say as I grudgingly pull away from her.

"I mean we can skip the festival," she says looking at me with haughty eyes. "Love, when did you get so horny. You pregnant?" I ask somewhat seriously.

She smacks my arm and I laugh at her. She rolls her eyes at me before getting up and heading to the bathroom.

"I wouldn't mind a little Jess, running around," I say a bit louder than normal as she was in the bathroom. "Not happening for a while, hun," she says sassily. "Mhmmm, we'll see about that, love," I call out.

I really wouldn't mind us having more kids. In fact, I really do want more kids. Maybe 11 more - If she knew what I was thinking, she would murder me.

"I love you," I called out. "I love you more," she responded. I scoff at her. "Why are you scoffing Mr Cole?" She asks sassily.

"Because, I love you more, Mrs Cole," I said, a grin on my face. "I love your smile," she says, looking at me intently. "Thank you, love. Our future children will get my smile," I say.

>>>>>>>>>

"It's so pretty," Crystal says as she looks at the decor. "It does look nice, my proposal decor was better though," I respond.

"Sure," she drags out the 'e' as she rolls her eyes. "You know... you'll soon be rolling your eyes when I'm balls deep in you," I say.

Her face reddens a bit before she smacks me, "Jess, we're in public, you idiot." I lean down and kiss her forehead then I adjust her hand in mine.

"How about we go grab some drinks?" I suggest. "Sure, I'm quite thirsty now that you've mentioned it," she says.

She got a pineapple soda and I went for a good ole Sprite. "Do you know who is performing?" she asks me. "I think Kheel, Marano brothers, Death Angels, Cherry Red, Ariel Kingsly, Cake and a few more artists," I say.

"I like Death Angels and Cake," she says, sipping on her drink. "I know, love," I responded.

"Awwww, you and your husband are so cute," squealed a bunch of teenage girls. "Oh, thank you," Crystal said, giving them a smile. "We're actually on our honeymoon," I added. "That's adorable," one of them said. "The festival is starting so, see you guys around," another said and the group left.

>>>>>>>>>

"Are you ready, baby?" Crystal asked, looking up at me. "Ready when you are," I say. "Yeah, I am, Let's head back to the hotel," she tells me.

We walked back to the hotel in the cool evening breeze. We're just talking to each other enjoying the moment.

>>>>>>>>>>>

I pull off my shirt and stripped down to my boxers. Crystal was in the bathroom, so I just climbed into our bed and turned on the Tv.

I flipped through the channels looking for something good. Deciding on the originals, I put away the remote.

Not long after, Crystal emerges from the bathroom. "Are you tired, baby?" I ask her. She shakes her head and joins me under the covers. She rests her head on my chest and I wrap my arms around her waist.

After a few minutes, she gets up and straddles my lap. She lays her head back on my chest and my fingers run through her long hair.

She eases off of my chest not much longer and kisses me. I fix my position and sit up more not breaking the kiss.

Spicy Content

She then starts to slowly move her hips. I'm pretty sure she can feel Jess jr down there as I'm only wearing boxers.

She breaks the kiss only to pull the skimpy, silk nightgown over her head leaving her bare and nude. My fingers slip down to her wet heat as she latches her lips unto my neck.

My fingers glide over her pussy lips then I find my way to her clit. I rub the sensitive bud slowly at first. She lets out a breathy moan begging me to go faster.

"Say please," I urge her. She rolls her eyes at me but complies. "The next time you will be rolling your eyes is when I'm making you cum so hard, you won't be walking for days," I tell her lowly.

I pick up my paste, my fingers rubbing her clit rapidly. She holds onto my shoulder for support as I rub it harder. She's moaning so much that she can hardly say a proper sentence.

"Look how wet you are, my love," I say as I hold up my fingers that are covered in her juices. She watches me with hooded eyes as I slide my tongue over my fingers, lapping up her juices.

I don't waste any time and slide my hand between her legs. I run my fingers over her slick folds and then slide two fingers into her.

She takes in a sharp breath of air as I plunge my fingers in and out of her. Soon her moans fill up the entire hotel room.

"You ready to take me, love," I ask, sliding my fingers out of her pussy. "Yes, hurry," she says breathlessly.

"Lay flat on your back and spread your legs for me," I say, in a commanding tone. She quickly does what I say. I slide my boxers off letting my member free.

I angle her legs over my shoulders and then slide into her wetness slowly. I go faster once I feel her clench around me.

My thrusts got harder and faster, her taking me whole. "I'm going to cum," she said moaning. "Let out love," I say speeding up so she can finish. Seconds later, hot liquid covers us and then I release into her.

"You better not get me pregnant," she says once she was able to catch her breath. I smile down at her, "No promises, my love," I tell her.

Chapter 32

3rd Pov

"Come on, baby, just one more push," Jess tells crystal as he wipes the sweat off her forehead.

Crystal lets out a pained hiss as her whole body clenches. Soon, the little cries of a baby fill the delivery room. "Take a breath Mrs Cole, we have one more child to deliver," says the obstetrician.

Crystal grips Jess's hand tighter as she follows the doctor's instructions. She's been in labour for the past fourteen hours and the pain hurt like a bitch even though they had put her on Epidural.

She pushed a total of 23 times before the 2nd twin was delivered. Crystal and Jess were blessed with a pair of boy and girl twins.

"Mrs and Mr Cole what are you naming the twins," asked a nurse. "The boy is Ezra," Crystal told her tiredly. "And the girl, Eveleigh," Jess continued. "Okay, Mr Cole will fill out a couple of forms while Mrs Cole gets some well-needed rest," the nurse says.

A nurse had placed the twins in a cot beside Crystal's bed while the other nurse was talking to them. Before Jess followed the nurse to get the forms filled out he had called in their family and friends to keep an eye on the twins while Crystal slept.

>>>>>>>>>>

"They're so beautiful," Crystal said softly while admiring her babies.

It has been six years since Jess and Crystal got married. After the honeymoon Crystal ended up pregnant and gave birth to a baby boy, Waylen.

Emily was excited to be a big sister and she adored her little brother from the moment her eyes laid upon him.

>>>>>>>>>

Crystal felt tinny hands wrap around her legs. She looked down to see Everleigh. She picked up the smiling baby in her arms. "Hi sweetheart," Crystal cooed at the baby. She giggled as her mom placed small kisses all over her face.

"Let's go find daddy at his office," Crystal told the baby. She went to Everleigh and Ezra's room to get the twins ready. Since Ezra was taking a nap she got Everleigh ready first.

Around 30 minutes later, she managed to get the twins ready, got ready herself and packed their bags. After closing the doors and making sure they were looked she got in her car and headed to Jess's office.

"Mrs Cole, you can't enter the boss's office, he's busy at the moment," said Jess's assistant. She looked at the assistant, her eyes roaming her face. She seems nervous - Crystal thought.

Being a doctor you pick up on certain mannerisms, so she ignored the assistant and went into Jess's office.

The sight she saw caused her heart to drop to her tummy. She saw a woman sprawled out on Jess's table with him between her legs. What made it worse is that she recognized the woman. It was the woman Kyle had brought to that Mexican restaurant years ago, Mariah.

Crystal gripped her babies tighter and stormed out of his office. Ezra and Everleigh could sense their mother's distress and they weren't happy.

Crystal didn't allow herself to cry in front of him but when she got to their house, the dam broke. She was happy that the rest of her kids were at school and that the twins had gone for a nap.

Crystal stood in the middle of the closet that she and he shared. She let out a harsh breath of hair and then started to remove her things.

What hurt her, even more, was that he didn't even bother to follow her out.

She called her lawyer and told him to draft up divorce papers then she called her best friend.

Jayla was livid. "The way how he looked at you, I didn't know he could hurt you like this," Jayla told Crystal. "I'm getting a divorce, we'll co-parent," Crystal said.

>>>>>>>>>>>>>>>>

Jess knew he messed up but he was going to try and win her back.

But what he didn't know was Crystal was completely done with him.

Jess went home after he finished his work and was greeted with divorce papers on the table. The house was dark and empty. He figures she had taken the kids with her. She probably went to Jayla's house - he thought.

>>>>>>>>>>>>

Crystal walked out of the courtroom with a smile on her face, she was granted sole custody. It was more than she had bargained for but she wasn't complaining. Jess did walk away with visitation rights and having to pay child support though.

"I will win you back," Jess said as he stared at Crystal. Crystal scoffed at him, "Stop kidding yourself, you look stupid," she said.

With that, she walked away from the man she was once so in love with.